W9-CLI-654

BRIDE OF AE

By the same author

The Devil of Aske
The Malvie Inheritance
The Heatherton Heritage
Whitton's Folly
Norah
The Green Salamander
Stranger's Forest
Daneclere
Fire Opal
A Place of Ravens
The House of Cray

BRIDE OF AE

by

PAMELA HILL

St. Martin's Press
New York

 For information, address St. Martin's Press, 175 Fifth Avenue, New York, N.Y. 10010.

Library of Congress Cataloging in Publication Data

Hill, Pamela.
Bride of Ae.

I. Title.
PR6058.I446B7 1984 823'.914 83-21293
ISBN 0-312-09540-6

First published in Great Britain in 1983 by Robert Hale Limited

First U.S. Edition

10 9 8 7 6 5 4 3 2 1

"It seems so *unladylike*. And the linen aprons are never the same again."

Miss Beatrice Wollaston sat mournfully in a chair in her kitchen, from which the maid, who did not live in, had departed for the day. At the sink was her niece Sara Ryder, unfastening the maligned apron. An assembly of coiled pots, mostly still not dry, stood near her by the oven. The room smelt of clay, and the late summer sunlight picked out more dust-motes than was usual.

Sara turned her head towards her aunt, and smiled, the smile giving her high-boned, rather sullen face a kind of magic, lighting up the green eyes to emerald and emphasising the thick, shoulder-length dark curly hair, which could never be put up without the assistance of pads for it would grow no longer. "You know very well, aunt," retorted Sara, "that I'd wash the aprons myself, but you say that's unladylike too." She ran some cold water into the sink and plunged the apron into it, watching with a kind of maternal pride the water grow milky with surplus clay. This had been a good morning; no brats at school, because it was Saturday. She'd made four pots, not bad ones, and after they were fully dried out Willum Hay would fire them for her in his lime-kiln. Willum did it for nothing if she sometimes gave him some of the pots to grow plants in.

On the stove the kettle started to boil, and Sara, after wiping her hands, made tea and set out the cups for herself and her aunt. She liked doing things about the house, liked doing almost anything anywhere, except—Well, that was what was making Aunt Beatie tearful today.

That lady surveyed her niece's stocky body, deftly handling the teapot and the cups. Sara's hands did not look either dainty or careful—they were too large, the fingers spatulate, and the nails always with a rim of dried clay underneath from her eccentric habit—yet Miss Beatie knew that, given a stocking or a gown to mend, she would do it beautifully. The dress she wore at the moment had been made by herself from a remnant of cloth for some reason left over, and although the small printed flowers did not suit Sara—she would have paid for bold dressing—the gown was beautifully finished and, as they said, could have been worn inside out. Her talents had not come from her mother—Mary Wollaston, who had surprisingly married a stonemason, had not, her sister remembered, been able to do much at all, a hopeless and helpless creature, who had typically died of pneumonia when the child was six—so it must be credited to Sara's father, that rough, outspoken bearded creature who had refused to permit Miss Beatrice to bring up the child after his wife's death and had done it himself. All of which accounted for a great deal, including the unfortunate incident to which Miss Beatie even now, two days after the event, dared hardly refer.

"You know that little Tommy Cunliffe's grandmama has taken him away from school," she murmured, as though passing the time of day. "At least she did not ask for the fees to be returned, but nevertheless I wish it had not happened. Other parents may hear of the matter, and do likewise."

"If Tommy Cunliffe had had his bottom smacked by his doting grandmama long before I did it, he might have become a reasonable member of society," retorted Sara, sitting down and sipping her tea. "This is hot; it's pleasant, although I'm sorry I didn't bake you griddle scones to have with it. But I did want an hour or two at the pots, and somebody else is nearly always in the kitchen."

Miss Beatie had winced at the word bottom, but it was too late, she knew, to cure Sara of her outspoken ways. Nevertheless she had a serious resolve in her mind, of which she meant to speak to her niece after tea; it was obvious that the project she had nourished, since the death of Sara's father two years ago, of taking her niece as a partner in the little dame-school would bring only disaster. Sara had no way with children; she could not understand that some must be cosseted, to please their mamas; she talked to them as if they were grown-up people, and often lost her temper. Although the days were, thankfully, long gone by when governesses were the least among the tribe of humanity and treated accordingly, one must remember that one was, more or less, on sufferance, and—

"Another cup of tea, aunt? Let me get it for you."

"Sara—"

"Yes, Aunt Beatie?" The green eyes blinked widely; they were set at the very slightest angle, giving the impression that their owner belonged to the tribe of Pan.

"You know very well what I have to say to you. The episode of Tommy was not the first—"

"No, aunt."

"—and if you stay might very well not be the last. If only you would control your temper!"

"It isn't temper," said Sara reflectively. "It is only that if they weren't chastised, as the Old Testament puts it, they would do the same thing again and again and again, and by degrees so would all the others, and we would all run raving mad."

"*I* have not run mad in thirty years of teaching."

"Then you must have the endurance of a rock."

Miss Beatie primmed her lips. "Sara, I have had a letter recently from an old friend in Yorkshire. She wants me to sell the school and come to share her cottage, where she lives in retirement, and help with the house and garden."

"Then you'll be a drudge all over again. Why not stay here?"

"Because I am, as they say, growing old. I cannot see myself going on indefinitely as I am, and I had looked forward to handing the school over to you. But it is evident that you are quite unsuitable, Sara, and I must sell it. I think that I can manage to do so, if I advertise in the right quarters. There is a very good magazine which caters for ladies' tastes; I would not like the school to be bought by anyone not genteel. It has—or had—a certain reputation, and I shall grieve to see it go, but I—" suddenly she laid her head in her hands—"cannot go on without help, and with all these catastrophes, and children being taken away."

Sara was by now truly contrite. She left the stool on which she had been sitting, and came and knelt at her aunt's feet. "Dearest Aunt Beatie, I have brought you nothing but trouble since I entered your door after Dad died. But there was nowhere else to go."

Miss Wollaston reached out a worn hand and patted the curly head. "I know it well, my dear, and was and am glad to have you, but . . . the money! Your father left none, and it has been a struggle to keep and board you even with the help you gave me in the school. And for you to go as a governess would be worse still, for you will not take insults quietly."

"Why should anyone?" muttered Sara. In spite of the fact that she felt sorry for her aunt, she turned her eyes to where the new pots sat on the sink-board. Was one beginning to list ever so slightly? It might be possible, if she went over now, to correct it, but—

"And so I have worked out a plan," announced Miss Wollaston. She clasped her hands together, cleared her throat, and watched Sara go over to the sink and straighten the pot. "Please, my dear, do leave your clay pots for a moment, and listen."

"I am listening, aunt." Sara surveyed her newly clay-stained palms; well, it would dry and she could brush it off. "A plan?" She smiled, and sat down in her place. The back door was open, and Samantha the tabby cat strolled in. What grace of body, what beautifully marked stripes, if one could render it in clay! Yet nobody round here would be interested in such a thing. But Samantha was always here, and another day when there was time to spare—

" . . . and so this Miss Edgeworth, whom I met once some years ago, is willing to take you as an apprentice for a hundred pounds, with a prospect of partnership at a later date. I have told her now neat you are with your hands, and she is delighted, because so few girls who come to her are other than clumsy, and some of her customers are of very high standing."

"Customers?"

"Yes, for millinery."

"*Millinery*? Oh, aunt . . ." She bent forward, and Miss Wollaston found herself unable to determine whether Sara were laughing or crying. Until she could decide, she occupied herself in thinking of the very hopeful vacancy at Brede-on-Sea, once patronised by the Prince Regent's acquaintance when he had used to come to Brighton for the season. He, alas, was gone, but a faint aura of gentility still announced itself from the headed writing-paper Miss Edgeworth had sent in answer to her letter. *Milliners to the Nobility and Gentry, and Lately to Royal Clients*. A small and obscure coat of arms had accompanied this statement. It would be an unparalleled chance for Sara; she herself had not the means to make the girl known to desirable parties for a marriage, and in any case, without a dowry, Sara would attract no one. The hundred pounds was not grudged, but Miss Wollaston hoped it would do.

"Yes, dear, millinery," she said firmly. "It is true that you will have unclassed yourself a trifle, but if you are diligent, and learn, you will prosper. And without money nobody can be anything at all."

Her things were packed; all she had she had managed to fit into a medium-sized straw hamper. Before setting out with Aunt Beatie to meet the post-chaise, which stopped about half a mile away on the main road, she went into the empty school-room alone.

It was all there, the familiar and hated smell of slates and chalk and ink and children. It has lost its identity as a room, just as, she reminded herself, Aunt Beatie had lost hers and become an instrument for pedantic instruction; at times it seemed, from her talk, that she could no longer rise above the level of the twelve-year-olds, the senior form. The desks sat in rows; opening one, Sara beheld the familiar sewing-samplers, which were one subject she had not minded teaching very much. She herself soon would become . . . what? An instrument for sewing on ribbons and feathers? What would Dad have said? But Dad, much as he had loved her, would not have had any practical sense about what to do in the present crisis and would have told her to do as she liked. How she missed Dad still, with his bear's hugs and his warm affection, and the constant dust from chiselled stone that got in everyone's hair, and the sight of great shapes coming out, slowly, painstakingly, where before there had only been granite or marble or sandstone! She herself had begun to chisel sandstone just before Dad took ill, and then there was no time for it any more . . .

Willum Hay had come today to say goodbye to her. "We

surely will miss the pots, me and the kiln," he said. Shyly, he produced a present he had made for her. It was fashioned of boxwood, and had one bevelled end and one plain, curved a little, at the other. Sara had known what it was; a modelling tool. Now, at some time, she would be able to use clay not only to fashion pots but to make heads, little animals, faces, every kind of thing . . .

She had thanked Willum with tears in her eyes. "I'll never forget thee," she said, in the country speech they both used to one another; and Willum wiped his nose with his sleeve, for tears were coming down it. "Nor I thee," he said, "and see an' make summat wi' yon."

"I'll make it, and fire it, and send it to you, I promise; just as soon as I know where I am down there."

"Tha should ha' stayed here," he said mournfully, and she watched him shuffle away. Was he right? But she would never have made a schoolteacher; never in this world.

The coach was full, and despite the fact that it had begun to rain slightly, a young man had to share the upper box. Before climbing to the perch beside the driver he kissed his wife, who was little more than a girl and wrapped in a shawl. Sara saw that she was soon going to have a baby. Not anxious to stare, she turned her head towards the window as the coach bumped along. She was thinking that, unlike other young women of her age, Dad had told her the facts of birth sensibly. It had happened when, bewildered, she had run to him years since because there was blood coming out of her. "Get a rag, and keep it there, and change it every day for five days," he said.

"But what is it?" She was less frightened than curious. Andrew Ryder had smiled, setting down his tools for once, and settling himself on the rim of the stone he was cutting.

"It's the way of the moon with women," he said. "You'd think the good Lord would have let them off with twice a year, like bitches, but no; it'll happen now every twenty-eight days until you're too old to be worth looking at. The only time it stops happening, unless there's something wrong with you, is when you're pregnant."

"Tell me about being pregnant." She had always been able to ask him anything; he never snubbed her or said a thing was improper.

"Pregnancy is when you're going to have a child, and for that you need a man. When a man and a woman marry the man's parts fit into the woman's, and if they do it often enough a child is conceived in the woman. The child grows and grows inside her for nine months, till it's ready to come out. Some women make a great fuss and screaming when that happens; your mother didn't. After the child's born the woman has milk in her breasts, and she feeds the baby until it's ready for other food. Remember all that, and remember that you must be married to the man you lie with. If you aren't, you'll make a fool of yourself and have a bastard."

She could remember his words as clearly as if he had just spoken them, and forgot the young woman on the opposite seat and began to think of Dad, and the great pieces of stone they'd had to sell to a different, inferior mason who bought them at a low price. She had not been able to shed the lost feeling she had had when first Dad's body and then the stones were removed, and Aunt Beatie had come and had taken her away in a hurry, because the school had been closed for a day so that she could come at all. After that, school; in and out of hours. At least she was free of it now. What would making millinery be like? To make anything gave a kind of satisfaction if one could do it properly. Making a baby must be the same thing.

She smiled at the pregnant young woman, who smiled back: she carried her burden with a kind of pride. The wet fields and hedges fled past, and now and again the post-chaise would stop, to collect and drop passengers and mail. At last they came within sight of Brede; Sara realised that she had never before seen the sea. It was grey today, and uninviting. But on a sunny day it would be blue, and perhaps in the evenings she might walk by it. It depended on Miss Edgeworth. What sort of a person would she be? Was she a relative of the author of *Castle Rackrent*? One must ask her.

Miss Edgeworth was waiting at the post-stage, her beady eyes, black as the jet she put on her mourning-bonnets, searching and finding Sara. The eyes looked her over, from head to foot and back again.

"You're Sara Ryder." The tight lips opened and shut again.

"Yes. And you're Miss Edgeworth." The woman wore a hat which did not conceal the fact that she dyed her hair and it was growing in grey at the roots. She wore an old-fashioned pelisse which concealed her figure, but Sara had the impression that it was plump and well upholstered, and moved stiffly. "Never mind who I am. We'd best get along," said Miss Edgeworth tartly. "Is that all your baggage?"

"Yes."

"Just as well. There isn't room for much. I've given you the right-hand attic. When you've unpacked your things and washed, come downstairs and I'll show you your duties." There was no mention of a cup of tea, and Sara would have been glad of one after the journey; she had managed to snatch a little light refreshment in an inn on the way, but that was all since breakfast.

They walked towards the shop, Sara thankful that her hamper was no heavier; Miss Edgeworth made no offer to help her carry it. The little town had a winding street, with two or three inn-signs blowing in the wind and rain. At present the street was deserted and everything looked grey. Perhaps it would be better when the sun shone, if she was allowed to look out at it.

There wasn't much time for looking out, and if it hadn't been for Aunt Beatie's hundred pounds Sara would on many an occasion have made her way back home. But what good would that do? She couldn't teach and didn't want to; she would not have minded helping to trim the hats which stood on little stands in Miss Edgeworth's front room and in her back, where there also reposed, astonishingly, a Russian samovar for making tea. Sara was not allowed to use the samovar, nor, except with a light duster, touch the hats. Also, she had to sweep and scrub the floors twice a day. When told of this her cheeks had flared red.

"My aunt paid you a hundred pounds to teach me millinery, not to scrub floors; I can do that at home."

"And you will do it here, or else go."

"But—"

"In a little while, if you have proved yourself to be clean and capable, you may sew the grogram on to the inside of the hats. But it takes far more to make a milliner than the three years in your indenture. You may count yourself lucky that you have been accepted in an establishment where there are no other assistants, all fighting for a place."

Sara, grunting with some amusement at the picture of a mill of young women fighting to scrub Miss Edgeworth's floor, went and did it. She had everything finished, thanks to her natural energy, long before Miss Edgeworth thought she would, and that lady was nowhere in sight; probably having a nip of gin upstairs with her feet up, thought Sara spitefully. She had not yet seen a single customer enter the shop, and had been strictly instructed not to say a word to them if they should appear; on the opening of the door a bell would ring, and Miss Edgeworth would appear like a guardian angel. So meanwhile Sara gazed on velvet hats, silk hats, hats with feathers and fur and flowers; their wide scoopy brims appealed to her awareness of shape and form; very few women would look plain in such creations. She opened a box on a shelf and peeped in; inside were feather trims, of all colours, some like peacocks' tails, others a mixture of pretty shades, one a brave scarlet that would have graced a soldier, another emerald green. Other boxes had more; there were ribbons in velvet and silk, of all colours, and a special box for mourning-jet as beady as Miss Edgeworth's eyes. In spite of the old lady she'd soon get to know what was in the shop, and where to put her hand on it.

The food was bad. For breakfast there was a hot cup of tea, thank goodness, but only bread and margarine to eat. It wasn't enough to sustain anyone scrubbing floors. About eleven Miss Edgeworth made herself a mid-morning cup of tea, lingered over it and a few sweet biscuits, then instructed Sara to remove the cold pot and help herself to what was left if she cared to. By then she was so hungry that she did care to, and swallowed the cold bitter liquid and as much milk as was left. The biscuits were not left out but put away in a tin. Lunch was largely made up of potatoes, with a scrap of meat that did not always taste fresh. It was got ready by a girl called, inevitably, Biddy, who clattered away at the sink and stove and, if Miss Edgeworth were absent, talked in such broad Irish that one understood only one word in ten. But the goodwill was there, and Sara, who as a rule did not mind her own company and was used to it, was glad of the little maid's presence.

The time passed. Sometimes there was a customer, usually dull and fussy, trying on every hat in the shop and then walking out with the one she had selected first of all, or none. Sara began to understand what had turned Miss Edgeworth into a tight-lipped dispenser of bread and margarine and cold tea. The shop itself was just past the place where carriages would have seen it, passing; as it was, only those who already knew that it was there would come in.

One day a notable thing happened. Sara was flicking her duster in the front shop—the floor was done. Outside there was the sound of a carriage drawing to a halt, and presently the shop-bell rang. Into the shop walked the most beautiful woman Sara had ever seen in her life. She was tall, with a figure like Venus, fashionably bustled, and had golden hair becomingly set in a knot low on her neck, not over pads and rolls. It made her look like a Greek goddess. Sara's fingers itched to get at clay to put down those memorable, incomparable features for ever and ever; it would be worth firing such a piece, or even, if she had a chisel, carving it in wood. What sort of wood? Something smooth, even—no knots—beech perhaps, or yew. She stood there gaping at the vision, who said, in a voice disappointingly harsh,

"I should like to see Miss Edgeworth. Tell her it is Lady Helena Consett. I am in something of a hurry, so pray do not delay too long."

But Miss Edgeworth, summoned by a quivering of the air, had manifested herself already, dropped a curtsy and said "You may go now, Sara," in a voice like the cooing of doves. She then set about Lady Helena; what could she do for her today?

"I want something simple, to wear to an *al fresco* at Overton. The colour is of no importance, but it must stay on if there is a breeze." Miss Edgeworth rushed to where several hats on stands might be covered by this description; but Lady Helena was not to be tempted. "No, no, plainer than that. If you have nothing I shall have to go elsewhere. But I was passing here, and decided that I would look in and perhaps save a further journey to town."

Sara, who had flattened herself against the wall in the inner room, was meantime observing a most interesting phenomenon through a little side window that gave on to the street. Outside, in charge of an elegantly equipped and polished phaeton drawn by two obviously pedigree bays, was a gipsy. He wore a tasteful livery in dark green, with a touch of braid here and there and a spotless white cravat upholding his swarthy neck; but he was still a gipsy. Even as she stood there second sight prevailed upon him and he turned his head and saw her staring, and winked.

Sara was prevented from replying suitably—she was in such a mood by now that she would have winked back, if only for a little diversion—but Miss Edgeworth, like a whirlwind entered the back shop, dumped aside the samovar, and dived into a large box which was secreted behind it and which even Sara had never seen. It proved to contain all manner of plain hats. Miss Edgeworth helped herself to a selection, hissed to Sara to put the lid back on the box and keep out of the way, and returned to the almost instant reply, "Oh, no, I don't think anything there . . . I'd better . . ."

In that moment Sara did a daring thing; perhaps it was the stimulus of the gipsy's wink, or perhaps merely that she was bored. There was a hat Miss Edgeworth had left behind in the box that would be just right. It was dark green velvet, with a long heron's plume. Set sideways on that head, at an *al fresco* party it would be—

"Excuse me." She was all sweetness and smiles as she entered the front shop, carrying her prize. "Don't you think that perhaps *this*—" and she twisted and turned the hat, showing it off to Lady Helena. "It would stay on in quite a high wind, and would be most becoming." And would match the coachman's livery, she thought, while saying nothing about that; but she knew, as if someone had taught her, how the minds of persons like Lady Helena worked, and she would see herself as part of a picture, arriving subtly underlined at the *al fresco*.

Lady Helena tried on the little hat. Miss Edgeworth was speechless. "If she doesn't buy it, there'll be the devil to pay," thought Sara. As it was, the woman made play to have thought of it herself. "A little more at an angle, perhaps . . ." and she tried to adjust it, but Lady Helena Consett waved her away. "Yes, I like it," she said critically, with narrowed eyes, thinking no doubt of the gown it would go with. "It will be like nobody else's there. How clever of you, my good girl, to find it! What is your name, pray?"

"Sara Ryder."

"*My lady,*" hissed Miss Edgeworth, prodding her assistant in the back. But Sara had decided to ignore Miss Edgeworth. This was *her* sale. Lady Helena Consett smiled a little, revealing—there was no doubt that it was a rabbit mouth—slightly uneven, but still white, teeth, and stared at Sara for a long moment with eyes that were an incredible gentian blue, if a trifle narrowly set.

"Well, Sara, there is a florin for you. I will take the hat. Will you have it packed and ready for my coachman to call for it tomorrow? Or I may come again myself; I haven't decided." She picked up her own hat, set it on, smoothed her gloves elegantly, and rose and went out with a swish of silk. No sooner had the door closed behind her than Miss Edgeworth started on Sara.

"*My lady* is what you must say, when addressing a titled customer; or else madam. Never, *never* stand in the stupid way you were doing, as though you were as good as she was. I never—"

"But I am as good as she is," said Sara stoutly, remembering Dad's brief phrases on the equality of man. The jet eyes smouldered.

"I never heard more! But for the fact that you have made a sale, I should seriously think if returning you to where you came from—and what they taught you *there* I can't think. As good as Lady Helena Consett! Why, she is the daughter of the late Earl of Middleton, and they would have married her to the master of Ae here, only the money raised some difficulty and they made the match instead with Mr Walter Consett, the other one's cousin. And now please put all these hats back in the box and remember what I have said. Familiarity will do you no good at all, and may lose you your situation."

A few days later Lady Helena swept into the shop again, but this time she was accompanied by a gentleman. And what a gentleman! He was beautiful—in the same way as Lady Helena, with fine high-carved bones and a classic nose and chin, but his hair was dark, his mouth straight and his eyes, on the one occasion when they swept over Sara, brown and rather ill-tempered. His clothes were a dream, consisting of a spotless broadcloth riding-coat of superfine quality, well-polished boots below breeches which had been chalked to a degree, and a stock whose tying must itself have taken an hour. He also carried a riding-whip, and so must have accompanied his cousin at an unplanned moment.

This time Miss Edgeworth was present. "My lady—Mr Francis—what a pleasure! What may I do to serve you today?" As she gushed she jerked an unseen hand at Sara, telling her to go away; when Sara did not budge, she spoke up. "You will no longer be required," she said. "Go to your place, and wait there."

"But I want Sara particularly to serve me," said the Lady Helena. Sara's smile, which was seldom seen, split her face in a grin, revealing even and very white, widely spaced teeth. "Come over here, my child," said my lady. "Bring me *that*"—and she pointed to a crimson silk hat with a pink rose garnishing it, and a confection of ruched net to balance the whole design. Sara obediently fetched it, doubting whether it was her ladyship's colour, but her opinion had not been asked. The result, on Lady Helena's golden hair, was disastrous.

"You see what pains I go through for you?" said Lady Helena mysteriously to the morose gentleman, who sat meantime in a chair, tapping his whip against his boot-top. He raised a peaked eyebrow, but did not smile. Presently his glance returned to the floor.

"We have a rather better one in blue," said Sara. "It would set off your eyes and colouring."

"You are gently spoken," said Lady Helena suddenly, taking off the crimson hat. She smoothed her hair with elegant, long-fingered hands on which were many jewelled rings. "How do you come to be here? How long have you been here?"

Sara reckoned incredulously, and found that she had been with Miss Edgeworth three months. She stated the fact, while leaving out the story of her arrival; she was not very proud of it.

Lady Helena did not appear to notice. "Do you like it here?" she said suddenly. Sara shook her head, unaware, and uncaring, if Miss Edgeworth, as was probable, were watching and listening from some alcove of her own. "Would you like another situation?"

"It would depend on the situation. There are worse ones, and my aunt paid a hundred pounds to get me indentured here." Let the old woman hear that too, she thought; but still no thunderbolt dropped from the sky. Lady Helena turned to her cousin, who was still watching the floor.

There would be no difficulty over that, in the event," she murmured. Mr Francis—Sara was ignorant of his surname—did not answer, but shrugged. Clearly he was in a very bad mood. Lady Helena smiled radiantly, as if to clear away all doubt, dissension and mistrust.

"I will not try the blue hat today," she said. "Perhaps later on you will hear from me."

Hear from her? Well, at any rate it didn't matter about the blue hat. Sara watched Lady Helena replace her own most becoming edifice, stand up, smooth her skirts, and sweep out of the shop through the door which Mr Francis held open. There hadn't been time today to see if the gipsy was driving them; possibly Mr Francis had handled the reins of the phaeton himself.

"Well, Francis darling?"

"Well what?" He made pretence to keep his eye on the reins, held slackly in his ungloved hands. They were fine hands, brown with outdoor riding, shooting, walking.

"Pray do not be stupid, my angel. Isn't she better than any we have come across yet?"

"Does she smell?"

"No, she does not. I made a particular point of noticing, both last time and this, when she fitted me with hats."

"She is not very handsome."

"Angel, what do you expect me to find for you? The

Venus de Milo? Truly, Francis, I have spent a great deal of time on your concerns in this matter. I would be grateful for a little . . . co-operation."

"I loathe Uncle Nicholas; that is all I know. When I told him I wanted to travel, he took me on a tour of the Lancashire cotton mills."

"But Uncle Nicholas is dead, and if you obey this clause in his will you will have as much money as you need to travel to Ethiopia."

He moved restlessly. "Perhaps there may yet be an heiress—"

"There will be no heiress. You are rising thirty, and it has long been known in the London circles that as a *parti* you are not to be considered because of this lack of money except under Uncle's express conditions. If you had fallen madly in love with anybody, it might have been different—"

"I have never been in love with anyone except you."

She took the compliment, preening herself a little; she knew she had deliberately drawn it out of him. Making her voice almost plaintive, she said "And Nigel? Nigel has lent you a great deal of money, as you know. He is the most patient and kind man in the world—"

"God, Helena, don't!"

"—and I do think, as his wife, that it is time he was repaid even some of the loans he has made to you over the years so that you might live as . . . a gentleman." Her gentian-blue eyes took in the immaculate appearance of the man beside her, his handsome profile, and she sighed a little. It would have been diverting to have been married to Francis. It would be less diverting, and give rise to gossip all through the county, to become his mistress, and she had never allowed it to happen; their relations were kept on the coolest scale, just enough to keep him devoted to her, a constant escort, and no marriage he ever made need alter that. Helena knew very well what she was doing.

Francis Atherstone's expression had grown grim. "If it must be done . . . and if only because of Nigel, it shall be . . . as you say, he's been good to me; most men would have sent me packing—"

"He was grateful to you for permitting me to marry him," said Helena smoothly. "After all, we could have run off together."

"And lived on what?"

"That, my darling, was the trouble at the time. If it had not been for that—had you even possessed a reasonable competence—"

"But I did not." He was gazing hungrily at her, the brown eyes lit from within by a red spark. "Helena—"

"Do you think," she said evenly, "that as we have at last seen a young woman who would not precisely revolt you, and who might even sustain her position well enough, we should visit the lawyer straight away? Then you could leave the rest to him, and not be troubled with it."

"To have another woman there—in the house—"

"And in your bed, a least for a little while. One has to face up to such matters; but it may not take long. She seems sturdy and in good health. Now, Francis, you cannot bury your head in your hands while you are driving those horses; make the decision, then we'll go and see old Probus. Why do lawyers have such names? One never meets with them elsewhere."

"You force me," he said faintly. "You force my hand."

"For your own good, I assure you. Think how pleasant it will be to be able to indulge your lightest whim—to travel, alone if you wish—to purchase whatever you choose. Think of the thousands the old man must have amassed in his time in India, and afterwards! What good fortune it is that he did not leave it to the spinners in the Lancashire mills!"

"There is that, certainly," said Francis Atherstone.

Sara received the letter while she was doing her first, pre-breakfast scrubbing of the downstairs floor. She had on a drugget apron and wiped her hands on it before taking the bundle from the postman. The rest were, alas, bills for Miss Edgeworth for those feathers and fripperies and trimmings.

A letter for her! And it wasn't in Aunt Beatie's handwriting. The envelope was on expensive paper and had a firm's name in tiny letters on the back. Well, best to get on and open it; the old girl would be calling from upstairs any minute.

She opened it, and read.

At first her mind was bewildered, though the message seemed clear enough. If she would call at her early convenience—that meant today, and Miss Edgeworth could lump it—they had a communication to make to her which she might well consider to be in her favour.

Might well consider? Well, either it was or it wasn't. Why couldn't they say so? Lawyers were so cagey. It *was* a firm of lawyers; below the heading it announced that they were also notaries public and commissioners for oaths.

"What are you doing, Sara? That floor should have been finished long ago. Was that the postman just now? You can bring the letters up, and then go back and finish."

While the tea gets cold, you old cow, Sara thought inelegantly. She took the mop and whizzed round with it, leaving everything presentable enough. Then she took the cleaning-things back to where they were left, put her drugget apron beside them, and ascended the stairs. She handed Miss Edgeworth her packet of bills and that lady glanced suspiciously at her own, which was held in her hand.

"What is that?" she said.

"A letter for me."

"From your aunt?"

"No." Sara went and poured herself tea. Thank goodness, it was just right for drinking. How she remembered the old tin mugs they'd used at Dad's shop, the tea so black you could dance on it, and loads of sugar. Now—

"If it is not from your aunt then I ought to see it. I am responsible for you here."

"I will tell you precisely what it says, Miss Edgeworth. Today I am to go to a firm named Buckler, Winstey and Todd to hear news to my advantage."

"To your advantage?" Miss Edgeworth made a grab at the letter, was eluded by Sara, who whipped it behind her back—the old bitch wasn't going to get her sights on it—and suddenly assumed a stiff dignity, seated in her chair.

"You may have an hour. They are situated at the other end of town. While you are out you may as well fetch me some black and some white sewing thread, and a new packet of large-eyed needles. My sight is no longer able to cope with the smaller ones."

"If they want me for an hour and ten minutes I'll have to take it," said Sara innocently.

"You are becoming very impertinent and stubborn. I have been too lax with you. Whatever it is you are to be seen by them for, pray do not involve me. I have enough trouble with . . ." Her voice tailed off as she recognised the hand of one of her most assiduous creditors, a lady who made artificial flowers in Clapham. Fortunately there was the money Miss Wollaston had made available. Miss Edgeworth frightened herself when she thought of the rate at which it had already shrunk, and business was not at all good.

"I shan't involve you," said Sara gently.

The offices of Messrs. Buckler, Winstey and Todd had been in the same red-stone building since before Waterloo year, and the first young Buckler had been killed in action. His portrait, gay in bearskin and scarlet coat, hung in the hall, casting a spurious gaiety over everything else, which left to itself would have been yellowish grey and curled at the edges. The present Buckler, who was in fact his nephew, was yellowish-grey also; skin, hair, clothes, all had the pall over them, and he maintained the no longer modish mutton-chops to garnish his colourless cheeks like pie-frills.

"Miss Sara Ryder," he repeated after the clerk who had ushered her in. Behind his colourless pince-nez he suddenly gave her a very sharp glance indeed. "Will you not be seated, my dear young lady?"

Sara sat. Unlike many young women of her age she was never ill at ease in any company, and found the old gentleman diverting and, in his way, pathetic. It was as though all his youth and colour had been sucked away by the inexorable demands of his profession. Behind him, on shelves, reposed an infinite number of black japanned boxes with white lettering turning yellow. She supposed they contained wills.

Mr Buckler had himself sat down and, clasping his long hands together, addressed Sara. "Where are your parents, my dear?" he asked.

"Dead."

"Ah. You are at present employed by Miss Edgeworth as

milliner's assistant along the High Street. Do you find the work congenial?"

"No. I wouldn't mind if it *was* millinery, but all I do for her is scrub floors and wash out the teapot."

Two unexpected, long dimples aipeared in Mr Buckler's cheeks. "I take it, then, that you would not be averse to leaving?"

"Averse? I'd jump at it. But my aunt, who is in Yorkshire now, paid a hundred pounds to have me taken on, so I can't leave; she hasn't much money."

"That aspect could be taken care of," said Mr Buckler carefully. Sara suppressed a sigh of joy, remembering. Even if it were taken care of—and by whom?—what would she do instead? All she ever wanted to be was a potter and sculptor, and there wouldn't be any money in *that*, not for a female. Willum and she had often discussed it, back at the lime-kiln when she'd turned some good pots out.

"Who would take care of it," she said, "and why?"

"That is a very long and involved story. I will keep it as brief as I can. You may recall that, some days ago, Lady Helena Consett visited the shop, and later she returned and brought her cousin, Mr Francis Atherstone, with her."

"I remember." All the time he spoke, she felt that she was, in a way, being tested. He'd looked pleased when she understood words like congenial and averse. Perhaps she'd try a few on *him*. What about prestidigitation? But it would be difficult to bring it in. Best relax.

"Mr Atherstone is squire of Ae, one of the oldest—though not the largest—properties in England. Its particulars go back to Domesday Book."

"It's certainly a queer name. Couldn't get much shorter."

"A fact upon which the Ae squires have always taken pride—even the late Mr Nicholas."

He looked down at his fingers. "Mr Nicholas was the uncle of Mr Francis, and the two did not deal well together," he said carefully. "All of Mr Nicholas' sympathies were with the working classes and the injustices under which they laboured. He was in his day an ardent Chartist and disciple of Cobbett. It might have been expected that, when he died, he would have left his considerable fortune—he worked for the East India Company for many years—to the poor of the district, or a fund for setting up workers' cottages, or some such thing. But he left it all to his nephew Francis, on certain conditions."

The old man cleared his throat and suddenly colour mounted to his face. "I hope—I really do hope and trust, my dear Miss Ryder, that you are not about to take offence at what I have to say. Believe me, it is necessary, and but for it I would not have brought you here."

Sara bowed a little. "I shall not take offence, Mr Buckler."

"That is charming of you. Now—the late Mr Nicholas left his entire fortune to Mr Francis in two separate lots, one when he married a woman of the working classes and secondly when she bore him a living son. The terms were quite clear. It is an unusual will, no question of it; I think he thought of it partly to tease his nephew, who would otherwise have married some young lady of conventional breeding from the shires. No!—your pardon, he would not. Had there been any money available to him, he would have married Lady Helena Consett, with whom he had long been on affectionate terms. But her father, the Earl, who was one of the old school, forbade the marriage for lack of the money, and married his daughter instead to another friend of the couple, her own cousin Nigel Consett. They share the House of Ae. I say all this so that you may understand, if you accept the offer, what things really are like. It would not be easy for any bride, and although you fulfil the expressed conditions you have already shown yourself, if I may say so, to possess both sensitivity and breeding."

"You mean that *I*—" Her mind boggled; to be married,

actually married, to the bad-tempered thoroughbred in the chair!

"Yes, Miss Ryder, I mean exactly that. Lady Helena in particular has searched for a very long time for a suitable working girl, but until coming across yourself, quite by accident, the other day, has not found a single one suited to Mr Francis' particular tastes."

"*I'm* not suited to his tastes. All the time he was in the shop he simply stared at the floor."

"Which you had just scrubbed, remember," said Mr Buckler, and the dimples appeared again. In fact he's an old dear, she thought, but this proposition—I don't know, I—But would it be any worse than Miss Edgeworth and cold tea?

"Would you like a little time to think the circumstances over, Miss Ryder?" Mr Buckler suggested gently.

She took a deep breath. "No," she said. "I don't need time. It isn't perfect, but it's the best bargain I've struck since I sold a flowerpot to Willum Hay's sister-in-law for sixpence, and she was as mean as they come."

"A flowerpot?" Mr Buckler was eager to keep up, but puzzled.

"Yes. When I can get the clay and somewhere to fire 'em, I make pots. I haven't got a wheel, though; I'd like that. And sometimes I carve, when there's the proper wood. Lady Helena's head; I'd like to do that in boxwood. It's so smooth, and the bones are there. And Mr Francis wouldn't make a bad job either," she added hastily.

"Miss Ryder," said Mr Bucker, "if you are sure—quite sure—that you accept the offer, I myself will give you the best wheel available for a wedding-gift."

"That settles it," said Sara.

After she had left the offices she wandered in a daze down the street, completely forgetting Miss Edgeworth's black and white thread and needles. Presently she saw a tea-room and stared in at the window. There were little iced cakes on stands, and it looked pretty and clean. That time Lady Helena—and it wasn't so long ago—had given her a florin she had gone out afterwards and bought a meat pie and eaten the lot. There was still some change left. She'd go in and have a cup of coffee and a cake, perhaps two, and think. There wouldn't be any peace for the latter exercise once she got back to the milliner's. She must work out exactly what she must say to Miss Edgeworth.

When she emerged, fortified and still with threepence left, she knew exactly what to say and do. She didn't hurry back to the shop, but dawdled along, staring in at all the other shop windows, thinking how her clothes, especially the underwear, were fairly shabby, though clean. Nothing had been said about it, but surely they'd give her some spending-money once she was married. Married! It'd make a cat laugh. If only Dad knew about it! She wasn't too sure that he would have approved; his views were more like those of Mr Nicholas of revered memory. Good luck to them both, wherever they were; and now she'd have to write to Aunt Beatie. Mr Buckler had told her not to trouble about the matter of the money with Miss Edgeworth; he'd see to all that for her. It was pleasant to have someone seeing to things, that is someone who could do it properly. They—she and Dad and later Aunt Beatie—had always had to pinch and scrape and scratch. Now, she would be Mrs Atherstone of Ae, with clothes she hadn't had to make herself. The thought made her swing her narrow skirts with pleasure, and it was while engaged in this occupation that she came to the door of the millinery shop and went in. Miss Edgeworth was sitting on the extreme edge of the customers' chair in the shop, and looked extremely angry.

"You have been gone for two hours and a quarter. Where have you been? The lawyers cannot have kept you all that time. I will not be taken advantage of in this manner."

"You won't have to be, Miss Edgeworth. I'm leaving."

"Leaving? You cannot. You are indentured to me."

"That will be seen about," replied Sara *à propos* Mr Buckler. "And I'm not going to scrub your floors any more. I don't mind doing a bit of dusting for you here and there, but that's all."

"You—"

The shop bell tinkled and a customer came in, one of the kind that would take a long time. Sara vanished from the scene and went upstairs, and just in case of emergencies ascended to her attic room and packed her few belongings into their hamper. If Miss Edgeworth actually put her out on the street she'd go back to Mr Buckler and say so, and he'd lend her enough money to stay at an inn. It was pleasant to have powerful friends.

Dear Aunt Beatie,

This news will surprise you, I hope pleasantly. I am getting married on Wednesday at the parish church here at two o'clock. If you would care to make the long journey down, please come. The lawyer is giving me away. It isn't a grand wedding and we haven't asked guests, only the family. I will write to you again soon and tell you how everything went off. In future my name and address is Mrs Atherstone, House of Ae, Brede, West Sussex.

I hope that you are in good health and that the new cottage agrees with you. Please give my kindest regards to Mrs Bolland.

Your ever devoted niece,

Sara.

There, that would do. She hadn't said anything about the hundred pounds. It would make a nice surprise for Aunt Beatie if she could send it back later, if that old bitch would part with it. But Mr Buckler had said he would see what he could do. Miss Edgeworth hadn't been invited to the wedding. It had been on the tip of Sara's tongue to do it, but the old girl had cut in and announced, very crossly, that she had no intention of attending as she couldn't leave the shop.

My dearest Sara,

Your letter has alarmed me not a little. I cannot believe that you have known this man very long. It would have done no harm to have waited until you had fulfilled your indentures, and then, if you still felt inclined, marry him. I cannot forget how your poor mother threw away the prospects of a career by so suddenly marrying your father, and I am certain it was the poverty of their conditions that carried her off. One can only hope that you will have better fortune than she, and I must end by sending you my warmest good wishes. I am sorry not to send a gift, but the premium for Miss Edgeworth took almost all I had and, as Mrs Bolland is not very well at this present, there is a great deal to do with medicines and visits from the doctor. She also sends her warmest regards and hopes that you are not making a grave mistake.

Your affectionate aunt,
Beatrice Wollaston.

Well, that makes a cheerful send-off, "at any rate, thought Sara. She put the letters away and went downstairs and did an hour's conscientious dusting for Miss Edgeworth. It was almost the last time she'd do it. She had remembered, at last, about the black thread and white thread and needles, and the haberdasher, Mrs Elmfold, had said she hoped it wouldn't be too long till they were paid for. Perhaps it would be kinder to let Miss Edgeworth keep the balance of the money. She must be in bad straits if she couldn't afford the price of needles and thread.

The marriage took place at the parish church. It was, Sara knew, far enough removed from Ae not to call in speculators who might gossip about Francis Atherstone's bride. For the same reason no banns had been called, Francis having searched his unthrifty pockets for the price of a special licence. He must be very much ashamed of his working-class wife, Sara thought, and was prepared to make her way down alone to where the small wedding-party waited by the altar. However the solicitor was there at the door, waiting to give Sara his arm; this was a great comfort and she never forgot it.

As they drew nearer—there was no music—she began to make out details. Prominent among the guests was Lady Helena, who wore a becoming outfit trimmed with sable, with sable-tails also on her hat's brim. Sara herself had no illusions about her own appearance; a letter from Aunt Beatie had made that clear. *I can spare you nothing more; there can be no question of a trousseau in such haste, as I think you might have known. You will simply have to wear the best you have. Try to obtain a little of the money back from Miss Edgeworth; she should oblige you, as she has not had your full board and keep to pay and you have worked for a certain time.* But it was like getting blood out of a stone to extract money from Miss Edgeworth; she would not part with a penny piece. She was losing an articled assistant, she said, and by rights should go to court. "You didn't contract for a scrubbing-woman," flashed Sara. She had left the good lady with her mouth full of pins working on somebody's hat, and hoped that the last remark would make her swallow them. For the wedding day, she had done as best she might, furbishing a shabby old velvet hat of her own with a stray feather in emerald green from one of the boxes. Green might be unlucky for weddings, but it went with her eyes.

They drew near. Beside Francis was a tall man with grey eyes; this must be Helena's husband. He bowed; the service began, and proceeded unremarkably. Sara felt no difference in herself for having promised to love and cherish Francis Atherstone, or for the prospect of being loved and cherished by him. From the unchanging expression on his face it was evident that the marriage-vows meant as little to him as they did to her, except that there would be no more floors to scrub. At the end of the ceremony Helena gave her a cool peck on the cheek, and the grey-eyed man, who had been groomsman, took her by both hands, smiling. He had not the classic beauty of Francis; his features were broader; but she thought he could be kind.

"I am Nigel Consett," he said. "You have already met my wife. As we will be sharing Ae with you, I hope that we shall meet often."

At the back, humble Biddy had crept in; they saw her as they went out. Sara turned back to speak to her. "Took the half-day off, I did," she said. "She'll carry on something frantic, but it was worth it to see ye wed, Miss Sara."

"If I ever need a maid, Biddy, I'll send for you."

The thin undernourished face flushed with joy. "Holy

Mother of God, is it meaning it ye are? I'll wait for the day, that I will."

The carriage-journey took them out of town and along one of the narrow older roads where two coaches could not pass one another. Sara found herself feeling tired, as if the effort of the ceremony had exhausted her. In any case it was all a sham; she had married Francis, and he her, for the same thing: money. She began to feel ashamed.

They were now deep in the forest, and sunlight filtered down through the branches with difficulty. "You will see the house round a sudden turn," murmured Nigel Consett, who during the journey had been the only member of the party to spare her a civil word; her bridegroom and Lady Helena were coldly taken up with each other after their usual fashion. Nigel began to talk about his daughter, Belinda, who would be waiting for them at home.

"She is . . . delicate," he said. "You will know more when you see her. She can only speak a very few simple words. But she is happy and good-natured." He did not say any more, and Sara wondered why they had not brought the little invalid with them; no doubt Lady Helena did not care to be seen in the company of a daughter who might channel some of the attention away from herself.

But what did Helena matter? The house itself was beautiful, and very old. It had that golden patina over bricks and timber which is oftener met with slightly further north in England, where the great folk lived in Saxon days. Part of this house was certainly Saxon. Different parts had been built at different times, but always time had come and merged the parts into one whole. Diamond-paned windows glinted in the scant sun. The forest reared behind, as if to make a backdrop in a play. There was a small oblong of emerald grass, very green. Nobody had made a garden.

"You like it?" whispered Nigel Consett in her ear. She clasped her gloved hands in ecstasy.

"It's lovely. It's lovelier than anything I've ever seen. It's lovely the way a good pot is, or a perfect rose, or—"

She stopped, and flushed. The others mustn't hear her talking rubbish. But Helena's husband gave a little bow and said "That has always been my own feeling for Ae, even though by blood it is not mine and never will be."

"I'd have sold the damn' place long ago if it hadn't been entailed," Francis Atherstone cast back over his shoulder. It was the first admission he had made that she was there. "That would have been wicked," she answered with spirit. "A place like this is to be—cherished."

"Well, Helena has been very good at cherishing it, and if you have any sense you'll let things stay as they are. She gets on with the housekeeper, and that's a big thing."

"Sara shall come with me for a day or two when I interview Mrs Padstow, and no doubt we can share the duties between us," interposed Helena sweetly.

Not on your bloody life, said Sara to herself with an expletive even Dad had only used rarely. It's my house, mine; I'm the wife of the master of Ae; I'll choose and direct my own housekeepers, thank you.

Inside the great door she could perceive men in livery and women in mob caps. From among them, a little girl ran out. Helena frowned.

"Miss Bartlett should not have permitted her to do that," she murmured. "She is becoming very lax."

Sara had been helped down from the carriage, whether by Nigel or Francis or the gipsy coachman she could never remember. A shock came to her when she caught sight of the little girl's face. This was Belinda, and she was an idiot. Oh, not the kind with small heads who make mischief, but an idiot nevertheless, with a smiling mouth and squashed nose and slitty eyes. It had a name, that kind of idiocy. The country folk called them innocents. And innocent Belinda was, aware of nothing but pleasure, laughing and looking from one face to another to espy her new aunt about whom she had been told by the governess.

Nigel embraced her. "How's my girl?" he asked tenderly. It would be easy to love the little creature. How old would she be, ten, eleven? Lady Helena had turned away and was peeling off her gloves. Sara went to the child and opened her arms, smiling.

"I'm your new aunt," she said. "Are you going to give me a kiss?" And Belinda ran into them, and kissed her; a sloppy kiss, followed by hasty cluckings and wipings as the governess arrived, a downcast young woman of the usual genre.

"You should have been here sooner," said Lady Helena coldly.

Sara made her way past the curtseyings of the women servants and the bowings of the men. She did not feel as overcome as she would have done, say, six months back. She'd seen a bit of life now, and a few kinds of people. By degrees, she'd establish that it was she who was mistress of Ae, and not her toffee-nosed ladyship over there. She couldn't be liked, not a mother who wouldn't speak to her own child. She—inside that shell of peerless beauty must be bones and rottenness, as Christ had said. One day Helena would be an old woman, and then it would begin to show.

And I? thought Sara, as she was led up to her room by the maid while a footman carried her hamper. They'd probably laugh at the hamper, back downstairs. Who cared? Everybody in Brede by now must know the story of the wedding, and how Francis Atherton of Ae had taken a bride from a milliner's shop.

The room was large, with an immense bed embroidered on its counterpane with a coat of arms, gold on green. The tester matched and had gold fringing, a Gothic spire at the centre and looped-back curtains. There was a rosewood commode with a ewer and basin in a floral pattern, and hopefully a matching chamber-pot in the cupboard underneath. Sara was beginning to feel the need of it. She dismissed the maid, undid her bodice and removed her hat and began to wash and comb her hair. She wouldn't change, because there was nothing to change into except the print dress she'd made herself, and the one she was wearing was better than that, shabby or not. If they didn't like her clothes they would have to buy her new ones, once the money arrived; she wasn't sure how long things like that took, and she wasn't going to ask Lady Helena, or her own husband either who wouldn't talk to her. No, she would ask Nigel Consett anything of that sort. He wouldn't be rude to her.

Dinner was served with candles glinting in their sconces at the four corners of the carved and polished table. Sara could not remember what she ate, except an enormous iced pudding which must have taken hours to prepare; it had cherries and angelica in patterns all over it, and meringue and whipped cream underneath. After the rigours of Miss Edgeworth's it would have done very well by itself, but naturally one didn't say so in so distinguished a company. As if to put her in the shade, Lady Helena had chosen a rose-coloured watered silk with a lace guipure, which made her hair shine in the candle-light. Francis Atherstone watched her almost pleadingly. Poor devil, it's hard on him, after all, thought Sara, and heard the bridal toast proposed by Nigel as though it were about someone else.

Afterwards, coffee was served in the French salon, as it was called because the furniture, gilded and upholstered in pale blue, had in fact been brought over just in time before the Revolution, by the Atherstone of that day. His portrait—he was quite a young man, and must have been making the last of the Grand Tours—hung above the fireplace, in which logs burned. Lady Helena sat down at the pianoforte and began to play. It was just as well, because until the men came back from their port there was nothing to say. Belinda had not been with them at the meal, which she probably took with her governess, and would by now be in bed.

The evening was short; as usual Nigel did most of the talking, as though to protect the company from silences that could not be bridged. Finally Helena—damn Helena!—said in her harsh tones that she was certain Sara must be tired, and she knew *she* was, and they had better all go to bed.

Sara looked round the company, smiled a little, and went out. She need not have troubled about the efficiency of the household arrangements. A maid was waiting to guide her back to her own room with an oil lamp, casting a soft glow on the stairs.

She got into bed and lay there, staring at the logs which had been lit here also and were now beginning to crumble. She still had the curious feeling that it was somebody else to whom all this was happening and that tomorrow she would wake in the attic room at Miss Edgeworth's, with the floors to scrub. Poor old girl—so greatly did distance lend enchantment—business wasn't good in that place, she needed to look for something much, much more in the public eye. Later on, as by degrees she, Sara, found her own feet, she'd try and help somehow. And as for Aunt Beatie's hundred pounds, perhaps it could be returned without robbing the old woman. They seemed to have plenty of money at least in prospect here. When it came, perhaps—if she'd done her duty, as some people put it—they would let her use it in that way; it wasn't all that much. Goodness, Sara Ryder—Sara Atherstone—your mind's got good and broad, hasn't it? The other day you were eating a meat pie from Lady Helena's florin and glad of the change.

The door opened and Francis Atherstone came into the room, in his dressing-gown. He carried a lamp like the one by which the maid had shown her upstairs. The shadows it made were flung upwards on his face, making him look like a devil. He did not smile. He set the lamp down on his own side of the bed and above it she could see the expression in his eyes, dark, contemptuous, and rakish. She lay still and silent while he put the lamp out.

Afterwards she was chiefly aware of a sense of outrage. He'd used her—he hadn't been kind, had said not a word, had handled her as though she were a wooden figure, then ridden her hard as though she were a mare. That's all I am to him, a brood mare, she thought. And—there was that also—she hadn't known how much it would hurt. People never told you anything. There was a deep throbbing in her body still, and she'd bled; they'd find the marks on the sheets tomorrow. After he had finished with her he had turned over and gone to sleep, apparently without difficulty. It had been like a mating of animals. She hated it, and hated him. But there was still Ae. She must remember that, and remember that whatever she had to endure from Francis Atherstone, he couldn't get on without her and must allow her something—something—of responsibility, power, whatever you liked to call it; after all, Lady Helena hadn't married him.

A stray thought came to her just before she drifted off to sleep; how much pleasanter if it had been Nigel in the bed with her, not Francis! But that notion would cause real trouble.

The days passed, and as Sara had foreseen the matter of her clothes came up, introduced one morning at breakfast by Helena. She sat pouring coffee—I should be doing that, thought Sara—and when the white, capable hand had set down the heavy pot she said, "Now that things are settled, don't you think that I should go to Brighton with Sara to choose her some clothes? One never knows who will call."

No one answered, and Sara, flushing, said, "I can go to Brighton by myself and choose my own clothes, thank you." And, she might have added, I can deal with the housekeeper and tell the maids what to do and keep this house looking as it does now, all without any help from you; you're a visitor. It was kind Nigel who rescued them all from the dilemma; Francis said nothing.

"Why do not we, all four, make a day of it and go in, and Frank and I can attend to some of our own business, you two shop and we can all meet for luncheon?" He turned to Sara, deliberately including her in the conversation. "There is an excellent inn at which we always eat—famous for oyster pies. And you will find as much variety in the shops in Brighton as you would in London; more so, because since old Prinny started the fashion of coming here at the start of the century the shopkeepers have always stocked up in time for summer, and I daresay the dressmakers too."

So it was decided, and Sara withdrew her ruffled feelings; after all it was pointless to nurse them when she could not speak to her own husband about the matter, only Helena's. Francis sill took no notice of her during the day, still came to their bed at nights, used her wordlessly, and turned over to sleep. She had become inured to it and, because he made no effort to be courteous, made none either. If she wept, she wept into the pillows, afterwards. No one knew.

The day dawned fine for Brighton and they made an early start, with a bottle of wine carefully wrapped in a napkin to aid them on the way. The gipsy driver—Sara had found out that his name was Runcatch, but could not have known, for he did not know himself, that this was a corruption of Hryncieiwiecz, which had been the name of his ancestors—mounted to his place in the larger coach, and they made off. Sara sat with her hands in her lap beside Nigel; she found solace in his company, even when they did not talk. Helena and Francis sat together as usual. How does Nigel endure it, Sara wondered? Poor little Belinda had wanted to come, but had been firmly forbidden, and she was partly consoled when Sara knelt down and said, "I will bring you a present from Brighton, Belinda."

The tears had dried. "What will it be?" the child said, in the almost incomprehensible nasal accents which were all she could use; one had to be accustomed to understand them. "Something pretty, perhaps ribbons, or a petticoat, or kid slippers; anything I see that I think you would like." The child did not understand half of it, but beamed because she was not entirely forgotten; and Miss Bartlett, the governess, smiled gratefully at Sara, because it was very seldom anyone paid heed to the little girl except her father. Mrs Atherstone was understanding and kind; so much so that she hadn't offered to bring a doll. Belinda was growing too big for dolls, and knew it.

The carriage bowled along until it came in sight of the steep slope leading down to Prinny's monstrous Pavilion. "We will show it to you in the afternoon, after the shopping's done," murmured Nigel. "He spent a fortune on it, and the kitchens are upheld by artificial palm trees, and there is a Chinese room."

"Not quite the same since the fire some years ago," yawned Helena. "But worth seeing, as you are here. Will you drop us off now? I want to show Sara the dresses Madame Rose will have to display, and if they are suitable we shall buy some. And shoes—goodness, we need everything. We will meet you at the inn, but do not expect us to be early."

The ladies descended, and into Sara's mind had come a resolution to be civil to Helena unless she deliberately tried to put her into ugly dresses. After all, Helena knew what occasions she might have to attend and, as she had already said, who might call.

Afterwards she was glad of her resolution. Madame Rose not only had gowns but silk stockings, underwear of the finest nature, rose-point nightcaps, and some millinery. Sara chose—and she did the choosing with only one slight protest from Helena that that stone-coloured velvet did not become her complexion, pretty as the gown was—six gowns in all, one for mornings in striped silk, a tea-gown, although such things were not her style, in floral wine-coloured chiffon, a *grande tenue* outfit in aquamarine blue, a walking-dress in emerald, the stone velvet, which had hand-made lace at collar and cuffs, and two casual dresses, one red, one grey. She also left an order for the making of a riding-habit. By now she was smiling and excited, and had forgotten all unpleasant thoughts about Helena; they went on to choose underwear, and a little straw hat, embellished with cornflowers and poppies, which would sit forward easily on Sara's thick hair.

Then there were shoes to buy; and a bedgown, which Helena said could be found in greater variety elsewhere. They chose a pale blue with blonde trimming, and then Sara said, "I must look for Belinda's present."

Her mentor frowned. "Do not trouble about her; she will have no recollection of having been promised one."

"But I promised it, and *I* recollect it."

Helena tapped her foot in impatience while Sara hunted through the articles in a shop which catered for children; in the end she found a beautiful petticoat, frill upon frill, with a threading of pale blue ribbon at the bodice and upper hem. "Of what use will that be to her?" said Helena. "Nobody ever sees her."

"She sees herself. It will give her great pleasure to have something pretty."

"Francis may object. He will have a good many bills as it is."

Sara drew herself up. "I think you forget that Francis is *my* husband," she said clearly, and deliberately went on to purchase a large box of crysallised fruits for Belinda as well. Helena shrugged and said nothing; she had no intention of a public scene with this girl they had had to marry to Francis. She did admit that, back at the dress shop, Sara had shown up well in the fashionable dresses; she was not pretty, not even handsome, but she had an air. However Helena knew she herself had firm hold of Francis, a cold determined grip that would not be relaxed as long as they both lived.

They returned to the inn laden with parcels, though not all; some of the gowns had to be altered and would be sent on. "Have you ruined him?" asked Nigel, jerking his head to Francis who at that moment had his mouth to a tankard of ale, and hastily jumped to his feet to salute the ladies' arrival. "I think we have been very careful, and chosen very well," replied Sara. She was still in a glow of satisfaction over the gowns.

"Except that I hope Francis will not mind paying for two expensive presents for Belinda," put in Helena, in the way of one who has come to the end of her tether in dealing with a difficult schoolgirl. Francis said nothing, pressed her to be seated and relieved her of most of the packages. "These shall go in the coach," he said, and went out.

"It was kind of you to remember Belinda," said Nigel softly. "Give me your parcels, in turn."

We are like a country-dance, Sara was thinking; cross hands, change partners. Nigel behaved much more like her husband than Francis did. Without him, she would be very lonely.

Some days later Sara, in the new striped morning-dress, came down early to the breakfast-room and resolutely marched to the top of the table where Helena usually dispensed coffee, pulled out the chair—there were no servants—and sat down. The heavy silver pots sat steaming by; she poured herself a cup, and sat drinking it thoughtfully and without helping herself from the array on the sideboard, which it was the custom at Ae to do informally and unaided.

Presently Francis came in; he had been riding. He glanced at her, laid his whip aside, and said, "That is Helena's place you are occupying." He made no comment on the striped dress.

"It is my place, not Helena's. I am your wife, or had you forgotten the circumstance? Certainly we have had very little talk since we were married."

"That is still Helena's place. I am the master here, and I say so." His peaked brows had drawn together into a heavy frown. Sara shrugged.

"Is Helena your mistress, then? Even so, your wife should take precedence, or so I have always been informed." In fact, nobody had informed her of anything of the kind; but she was not going to give way easily.

He flushed. "Helena is not my mistress, and never has been. She should have been my wife, but for the terms of the humiliating will which brought you here."

"Your time spent on me has not been entirely wasted. I am pregnant."

He gave a movement of pleasure. "That is—good news. I hope it will be a son."

"I shall try to arrange it. Will you have some coffee?"

She did not wait for an answer, but poured it in the way she knew he liked it—had she not watched Helena all these nornings?—and passed it to his place. Francis meantime had gone to the sideboard to help himself to kidneys, bacon and egg. Sara did not look at the food; in fact, the sight of it made her queasy. She had played her trump card, and it looked as if she might win this round; he had said nothing more about displacing her.

Presently Helena and Nigel came in. Helena raised her fair brows a little at sight of Sara in her accustomed place, then gave a light laugh.

"My dear, you could have relieved me of that task at any time; why did you not ask before?"

"Sara has news for us," said Francis. It was so unusual for him to speak, and in particular of Sara, that everyone listened with interest. After the congratulations were over Helena asked when the child would be born.

"Oh, not for a long time yet. February, I think."

"You should see the doctor, and find the exact date."

"Thank you, I know the date," maintained Sara.

One thing that had given her immense pleasure was the furnishing of her studio. It had happened the day after they all came back from Brighton, and she found that Nigel had bought a gift for her of everything a potter should need—clay, tools, trimmers, plaster, potter's smocks, a basin for water. Mr Buckler's potter's wheel had arrived some time ago and Sara had had it carried to a room which nobody seemed to need now, an old dairy at the back of the house, where there was a sloping floor and a drain. Some of the windows were broken and everything was very dirty, but she had already set the maidservants to cleaning it and had asked Runcatch—who seemed to have several talents—to replace the glass. Now, it was ideal; a great disused kitchen table held most of the gear, and there was room for drying pots. Having won her battle over the coffee, a little later in the day when she felt better, she changed into her old clothes, put on her smock, and went to the studio ready for work. The clay was covered with wet sacking to keep it moist. She cut a large slice with the wire cutter, slapped it on the scrubbed table, leant on it, twisted it, gave it the ox-head shape with her fists, twisted again, slapped, cut—and moulded the whole into a wedged ball.

Mr Buckler's wheel worked like a dream. She felt her foot, in its old familiar shoe, kick the lower weighted wheel and revolve the upper, seeing its anti-clockwise rhythm with a kind of delight. Soon she took the clay and, holding it above her head, slammed it hard down on the centre of the revolving wheel. Quickly dipping her hands in the water, she began to fashion a pot, feeling the clay rise and make a pyramid, then flatten, then rise again. She gave it the potter's grip and began to make the shape, while the sweet running of the wheel followed the obedient clay as it rose, narrowed, edged, refined, steadied under her hands. She took the trimmer and neatened the bottom rim, then the turner and neatened the top; then she stood back, happier than she had ever been in her life, aware of the child inside her and the pot she had made confronting her. At this moment, Helena didn't matter; Francis' coldness didn't matter; nothing mattered but creation, the whole of it, as God had made it long ago. Whatever befell at Ae, she would be able to come down here, work off her bad temper—they said one should either make a pot or bake a cake—and be with the clay. She left the pot to dry on the wheel; she didn't want to do too much today. Then she took the water and scoured the places the clay had fouled, with far more enthusiasm than she had ever given to the floors at poor old Miss Edgeworth's. They might have bought a hat from Miss Edgeworth the other day, while they were at it. One day, she would. But just now it didn't matter.

She rinsed her hands, left the potter's smock hanging to dry, and left her kingdom, with a backward glance. There was even a lock fitted to the door, of which she had the key. Nobody would come interfering and pushing about the pot before it was dry as leather. This was her place, her place; and so, she told herself fiercely, was Ae.

Nigel Consett reined in his horse deep in the woods, out of sight of the lichened roofs of Ae. He slid down out of the saddle and let the beast graze, his figure picked out by a shaft of sunlight which slanted between the erratic growths of the firs. Beyond was the valley, and Nigel rested his eyes on it; he needed desperately to be by himself for a little while, free of the need to keep up appearances.

He was troubled about his marriage. That might have seemed inevitable; he and Helena had not cohabited since Belinda was conceived, and after the child's birth she had refused to be a wife to him on the grounds that another monster might be born. She had no mercy in declaring that the fault came from his side, not hers; they had never had such a thing in the Middleton family. Consultation with doctors had provided Nigel with small consolation; these little creatures were born, for no apparent reason, gave no trouble, and did not live long, generally dying of a chest infection before the age of twenty. Nigel had been especially tender towards little Belinda, more so than if she had been an ordinary, intelligent child: Helena mocked at him.

"You are wasting your time. She understands nothing," she would say, on the rare occasions he, she, and the child were together. To think that he had once been delirious with joy—though of course sorry for poor old Frank—because the beautiful daughter of the Earl of Middleton had been promised to him as a bride!

He had soon found her to be frigid, snobbish, and completely self-centred. Yet she retained a certain witchery, so that Frank, who had been in love with her all his life, was in love with her still. It had not mattered till now; Nigel knew that Helena would never be any man's mistress. But now Sara had come, and Nigel felt his starved heart reaching out to her over her kindness to the child, her impulsive warmth, her complete lack of an eye to the main chance: in other words, she was in every way the opposite of Helena. As for her origins, at which Frank looked down his nose, they had been decent enough; the father had had artistry in him, and had passed it on to Sara; the mother had been educated, and had passed that on too. And Sara herself had an independence and dignity that enabled her to meet any new situation as it should be met; nobody could have taught her that; it was a part of her.

So he loved her, and admitted it. Should he and Helena leave Ae? Francis, lonely long ago, had appealed to them both to make their home there. "What am I to do with thirty or forty rooms thick with cobwebs, talking to myself till I go mad?" he had said. So Helena—there was no question of her taste—had furbished, draped, had the place swept and washed and polished. She had an obedient staff whom one hardly saw. Was he to disrupt all that because of the dictates of his heart? Never! Also, by staying, he might be able to help Sara in little ways; she had enough against her. Fortunately she seemed not to have let herself be dazzled by Frank's handsome looks, as many young girls would have been; she still called him—Nigel laughed in the midst of his pain—the Ill-Tempered Thoroughbred.

So what was to be done? Nothing; go on as they always had, but keep watch over himself. He had done it, after all, for many years in disguising the wretched failure of his marriage to Helena. It would be easy to hate Helena, accordingly, but he had not permitted himself to do so.

"Cloud," he called, and the horse, which was a dapple grey, moved towards him through the trees. He wondered if Frank would give him permission to teach Sara to ride. She could already do so a little, and there was no fear in her; but perhaps with the coming child it was better not.

Nigel found himself thinking with deep jealousy of the child Frank and Sara had made. To down it he leapt into the saddle and cantered down the bridle-path, using Cloud hard. Presently he must go into breakfast and meet them all and—he grinned suddenly—accept his coffee from Sara, who still presided over the pot. That had been one victory and there might be more.

Next day, a thin young woman carrying a bundle, and with her shoes tied up in rags, appeared at the back door of Ae to ask if she might have a word with Mrs Atherstone. The scullery-maid, who opened it, took one look, put down the apparition correctly as Irish, and said she'd better wait to see the housekeeper. That lady, Mrs Padstow, having been informed, sent for the Irish girl to come to her room and put a few questions to her regarding the reason for her visit.

"Well, I can say all that to Mrs Atherstone, can't I?" retorted Biddy, not in the least overawed by her surroundings, though to most of the servants except Runcatch the housekeeper's room was the annexe to the throne of God. "She said I was to come whenever I'd finished working where I was before, and she'd have work for me. That's all I'm telling you, and if you don't fetch her for me I'll go round to the front."

"You have a very good opinion of yourself, my girl. I will inform Mrs Atherstone that you are here, but as for fetching her—What is your name?"

"Biddy."

"Biddy what?"

"Biddy'll do." She wasn't going to be browbeaten by this old nanny-goat. Mrs Padstow pursed her lips and rang a small bell, which brought in a footman.

"You will inform Mrs Atherstone that a young woman calling herself Biddy is here, and would like a word with her if she can spare the time." The footman bowed, gave a telling glance at Biddy, and went to obey his orders. Oh, they needn't think they're anything, Biddy thought to herself as she stood there, not having been asked to sit down. When I see Miss Sara, she won't have changed a bit. It's a great big house she's come to: I hope she's happy in it.

The footman returned with instructions that Biddy might follow him. "Please do not leave mud on the carpets," Mrs Padstow called after her. "Your shoes are not clean."

Neither would yours be if you'd walked from Brede, Biddy told herself; but life had long ago taught her when to keep silence and when not. She followed the footman, who did not deign to address a word, along flagged passages, up a short flight of stairs and then to more passages, this time carpeted.

"The young woman, madam," announced the footman in tones of heavy distaste. Sara flew out of her chair and came and kissed Biddy on the cheek. It was well seen, thought the footman, that the new bride of Ae did not come from the best regulated establishments. He retired, having been waved away by Sara.

"My poor girl," said Sara, "you must have a cup of tea. This is fresh; I was drinking it by myself. Why are you here? Has something gone wrong with Miss Edgeworth?"

"Miss Edgeworth's dead, that's what's wrong with her. She was found sittin' in her chair sewin' grogram ribbon, and not a breath in her body. The funeral's on Tuesday."

"Oh, Biddy, and I meant to help her, and never did it. Poor soul. I shall go to the funeral, of course." Biddy's Catholic connections would frown on her going, so Sara said nothing of that. She watched Biddy gulp down the tea gratefully, and said, "There will be a good supper in the servants' hall in a little while. You are one of us now, if it suits you. I want a personal maid."

"A personal—" Biddy's eyes goggled. She had hoped for, at the best, a job washing dishes, the same as she'd had at Miss Edgeworth's. "Oh, Miss Sara—ma'am—it is kind, but I have no notion what a personal maid does for a body. I would make a fool of myself, and maybe of you."

"Do not worry," Sara assured her. "All you need do at first is sew on a few buttons, and perhaps do a little ironing of collars and cuffs. You can do that, can you not? And—Biddy—there is one thing I should like you very much to help me with. My hair is too short to put up unless I use pads, and I would greatly like someone to help me with the back of it. I'm sure you would do as well as anybody else."

"I will surely try my best, ma'am. And I have me best dress with me that I used to wear on Sundays, and maybe you could get me a cap and apron."

"Then that is settled," said Sara, and named a wage. Then she pulled an embroidered cord which sounded a bell in the housekeeper's room. In a few moments Mrs Padstow was with them, looking somewhat like a ruffled turkey.

"This is Biddy, who is going to be my personal maid. Pray provide her with caps and aprons from the store, and see that she gets a new pair of shoes. She will start at once, and will take supper with you all tonight. I know that you will make her welcome."

Whether Biddy was made welcome at first was an indecisive point; new servants seldom were, until they had learned the proper degree of respect among the hierarchy of scullery-maid, housemaids, parlour-maids, cook, footmen, grooms and Mrs Padstow herself. From the beginning that lady had a down on Biddy, but it was like squashing rubber. The Irishisms she came out with set everyone laughing, and despite Mrs Padstow's disapproval (and that lady was not liked for her own sake) the new maid was friends with everybody within a month. Also, she had learned some skills as regarded Sara's hair and clothes, for there was nothing she would not do to enhance the appearance of her beloved mistress. She passed many an otherwise lonely hour for Sara, with the two of them laughing over frills and pads. Mr Francis was not often seen, and was described by Biddy (to herself) as a gloomy gomeral. He had made no comment on the appointment, but supposed that after all women in general had maids; Helena had one, naturally.

Times had changed rapidly towards the end of the century, but what were still known as Polite Invitations arrived punctually and were placed within the rim of the mirror in the drawing-room. Here Sara had as much chance of studying them as anyone else. It so happened that since she had come to Ae the invitations were mostly of the male variety, generally inviting Francis and Nigel to a shoot; this was not hunting country. However, today a command had come which had intrigued and excited her when she caught sight of it; a *fête champêtre* at Daisyhill, the home of the Lord-Lieutenant, Sir Charles Kaye-Billington. It was made out for F. Atherstone and Party, and Sara reasonably hoped that she would be included as well as Helena. However a kind of obstinacy in her made her keep silent on the subject; she would wait till Francis mentioned it himself.

During the next few days Nigel announced that he must ride to London on business, and would be away till the end of the following week. This left Sara disconsolate; must she now trail through the *fête champêtre* behind Helena and Francis? However, she would do it. Nigel left, riding on Cloud, for he disliked the stuffiness of coaches. The house seemed inexplicably empty without him, and Biddy, seeing her mistress doleful, did her best to cheer her up, but if she had known, the most merciful thing would have been silence. The days passed, and still no mention was made of the coming party. Francis slept now in his dressing-room, which was a relief to Sara, but it made it more difficult to address him, and she was not sure that she would have done so even had he been in bed. She had got over her morning-sickness, and the child was not yet beginning to show; in fact, she had a pretty colour in her cheeks, and had never looked better.

The day before the *fête* she made up her mind. Francis had no intention of taking her. He would go in the phaeton with that bitch—it had probably been an established custom of theirs year after year—and would not even trouble to mention the matter to her, his wife. She longed to have it out with him, but after all she might lose the battle and be unable to go; as it was, she had a plan.

She sent Biddy to the stables. Was Runcatch going to be driving the carriage tomorrow? Alas, Runcatch was on his day's holiday. Was the phaeton going out tomorrow, then?

"And what do you want to know that for, Irish Biddy?" asked the groom, and winked. He and Biddy often had notable exchanges in the servants' hall, to the horror of Mrs Padstow. "Because I want to, and the reason's none of yours," said Biddy. "Me mistress's orders, then, are that ye clean up the ould pony trap and have it harnessed after the others leave tomorrow. We are takin' Miss Belinda for a drive."

It was Francis Atherstone's loss that he seldom if ever troubled to supervise the stables himself, but left it to the head groom. Provided his equipages were ready, clean, shining, and safe, he had no wish to know more. He had probably forgotten (but Sara in her forays had not) that there was, in the back of the main stable, an old pony-cart that had hardly been used since Francis' childhood, when he and his tutor used to go for drives. "Well, it's to be cleaned up proper now, and mind ye use saddle soap a-plenty on it, and see the girths ain't crackin'," Biddy informed him. He answered that neither she nor anyone else could teach him how to clean up an old cart; he knew all about it.

"And ye'd better, and the mistress in her blue dress and all," she flung at him, and sped back to Sara to tell her the command had been issued. Sara was almost enjoying herself. It would have been pleasant to go with Francis and Helena, and be properly introduced to the host, but if Francis did not want to take her he need not trouble himself; she would manage on her own.

The phaeton set out next day, a day of cloudless sunshine, with Francis at the reins and Helena by his side, in a huge flower-wreathed hat and peppermint dress; they laughed and chatted as they drove off. As soon as they had gone Biddy ran down to the stables to tell the groom to bring the pony-cart round. "Who's drivin'?" he said, anxious for the pony, who was staid and old.

"Who but meself, to be sure? I was raised on a farm, and there isn't a thing I can't do with a horse, is there, my colleen?" She stroked the old pony's nose. The groom watched, suspicious that something or other was going on, but after all Mrs Atherstone's orders were none of his affair. He brought the trap round to the front of the house, saw Biddy seated at the reins, and watched Sara, brave in blue, with the little straw hat tilted over one eye, descend the steps of Ae with Belinda by the hand. Belinda also was dressed in her best, even to the petticoat Sara had brought from Brighton, and she wore a round wide-brimmed hat to shade her eyes from the sun. She chuckled and smiled as she was lifted into the cart; the small sharp nipples of puberty were showing beneath her bodice, for such children matured early.

The cart set off. At first the modest pace drove Sara crazy; the party would be over before they got there! Then she began to be glad of the pony's steady trot; it would be safer for the child she carried. Biddy knew where Daisyhill was; there was very little Biddy did not know; all one need do was sit at ease while she handled the reins finely. "We must do this often," Sara said, and little Belinda laughed and echoed her. "Often," she said. "Do often."

If the master lets us, thought Biddy. Half of her eagerness in coming out was for the same cause as Sara's; that was a mean man, mean as a weasel, and he deserved what came to him.

The great gates of Daisyhill were open and the tracks of several carriages could be seen. On either side, on pillars, were emblems which had survived Cromwell's swordsmen long ago; stone greyhounds with collars of marguerites. They drove on, past the curtseying lodge-keeper's wife; her man was gone to help with the horses and carriages, which were by the lake.

Biddy headed for the place and was recognised at once, for several of the servants from other houses knew her. It will be all right to leave her, Sara thought. She herself was helped down by one of the coachmen, and Belinda lifted after her; she took the little creature's hand, which was warm and sticky with the heat. There was a pleasant smell of new-cut grass, and the avenue of old trees shaded the lake, by which several parties sat already consuming jellies and blancmange. The host, Sir Charles, rose from among them and came hurrying over to greet Sara. There was no immediate view of Francis or Helena.

"I see no sign of my husband, so I must introduce

myself," said Sara, looking the old nobleman in the eye. "I am Sara Atherstone, and this is Miss Belinda Consett. Belinda, make your curtsy."

Belinda bobbed, and Sir Charles engaged Sara in easy conversation while he took her by the arm to go and search for Francis. My word, won't he be livid when he sees who's bringing me to him, Sara thought. A little smile came to her lips and her eyes were green fire. Sir Charles approved. Damned handsome woman Frank Atherstone had married; one must see more of her. They kept themselves too close at Ae.

"And are you happy among us down here, my dear?" he asked, his grey moustache, of which he was very proud, bristling finely. Sara considered her reply carefully. "The countryside is very beautiful, and I love Ae," she said, "but I am a little solitary. It is delightful to have been able to come today. I waited behind for the trap to bring Belinda; she doesn't get out enough."

Charming person, Sir Charles thought; not many would trouble themselves about another woman's little mongol. Where was Helena Consett? Her toilette should be easily enough seen, God knew. "Ah," he said, "there they are; over by the oak. I'll come with you, if I may, and have a word with Frank, and then they shall bring you some of these delicacies we have here. They tell me the lemon soufflé is particularly fine."

Francis had seen her coming; of course he had. He struggled up as she and Sir Charles approached and his anger made him white about the mouth. They exchanged a few nothings, Francis was congratulated on his handsome bride, and then—and Sara knew a little sinking at the pit of her stomach—they were left alone.

"What the devil are you doing here?" said Francis in a low voice. "You had no business to come, and as for bringing—" his dark glance did not include Belinda; he could never endure to look at her. That Helena's beautiful body should have been racked to produced such a gargoyle! That was what the child was like; one of the gargoyles on Notre Dame.

Sara answered him coolly, sitting down and spreading her skirts on the grass. "The card said 'and party', so I assumed it would include your wife. And what harm is there in bringing Belinda? I will look after her, if her mother will not." There, she thought, I got it in. Helena's profile continued serenely undisturbed; she might have heard nothing they were saying.

"You—"

But the servants were bringing up delights from the table; game with the bones drawn out of it, set in aspic; ham and tongue, ice-cream, the lemon soufflé Sir Charles had recommended, all manner of other delicacies. Belinda squealed with ecstasy and grabbed at the puddings, until Sara said gently "No. The meat comes first. Take a little game, Belinda, and eat it prettily. You know how."

Neither Francis nor Helena ate much, though the latter toyed with a mouthful of soufflé. Presently other guests came up, shepherded by Sir Charles to meet Francis Atherstone's charming bride. Sara said the right things, made the right impression, made friends, was asked to visit here and there. "But you must come first to Ae," she said mischievously. "Now that I am here it will be a pleasure to meet everyone again. What a lovely day it is! How fortunate that there is no rain!"

She was stifling with laughter inside herself; but at the same time grateful to Sir Charles. These weren't the toffee-nosed people Francis would have led her to expect; they were kindly, and wanted to know her, and they should.

Afterwards, when they were home again and alone, he said to her, "If you ever play a trick like that on me again, I'll whip you from here to Brede. Stop sniggering; I mean what I say."

"That would do our coming offspring very little good. How disappointing for you if you did not get the rest of the money after all!"

He gave an oath, and flung out of the room. Much later she heard him coming up to his dressing-room, steps dragging; he was drunk. Hers had been the victory, like the day of the coffee-pot. All one needed to do was make plans.

If she had known how coldly angry Helena Consett had been at the public showing of her afflicted child, even Sara might have been a little afraid.

It was late at night, also, when Nigel returned from London; Sara was asleep and did not hear him arrive. Next day at breakfast Helena was absent. Nigel put down his fork and said in a low voice, "I had a thing I wished to discuss with us all present, but my wife chooses not to join us; the pair of you had best hear it from me. I have the option on Withenshaws, and propose buying it."

"And leave Ae?" cried Sara, while Francis looked at his plate. She fell silent; it was Nigel's affair where he lived, possibly he wanted a home of his own, and she would be glad to get rid of Helena, but . . .

Her eyes met Nigel's across the table. Without words, they knew their feeling for one another; it was as though the eyes spoke, green to grey. It is for that that I must not stay here, Nigel's eyes said. It is for that that I shall miss you as if they had torn out my heart, Sara's answered, and within her was surprise and grief; she had known she loved him, but not how much.

Francis raised his head. "I take it Helena does not approve of the plan?" he said. Sara might not have been in the room; he glanced only at Nigel. Nigel suddenly flung his head back.

"Helena will do as I say," he told them. "It is unfair to Sara to have two hostesses in one house; it is time she was mistress here."

"Nigel, do not go because—"

"Be silent," said Francis to his wife. To Nigel he said, with a tone of regret, "I shall miss you both. There was no need for it. There is ample room here."

Nigel lowered his gaze and briefly remembered the icy rage with which Helena had received his news. "You will be able to see as much of Francis as you wish, or he wishes," he had told her, and she had flung about like a Greek fury.

"What do you know of friendship?" she had flung at him. "You, who gave me an idiot child . . . are we to have *her* at Withenshaws? I will not have her under my eye all day; I shall send her to an institution."

"You threatened that before, and it shall not happen. The inmates are whipped and made to be a public show. If Belinda is happier in the place she knows, and with Sara who loves her, then perhaps they may permit her to stay here. Otherwise I myself shall have the keeping of her."

She had shrugged. "That is nothing. Francis and I, all these years, have been as close . . . almost as close . . . as if we had married. I should have married him, not you."

"Which is one reason why it will be courteous to withdraw to Withenshaws and leave him alone with his wife, and the child they are expecting."

"And if I refuse to go?"

"I will see that the law makes you."

He had an instant's vision of her, beautiful as evil, her loose hair flung about her head like the Medusa's snakes: he had come on her while she was combing it. "You upstart, to think to govern me," she had said, and slapped his face. He hoped the mark did not show red when he went down to breakfast.

Afterwards Sara said timidly to Francis, "You do not want them to go, do you? If it is for my sake, stop it. You will be solitary," and she did not add "without Helena." He walked away from her. "It is all your doing," he said. "Before you came this house was run smoothly and without quarrels."

"We have had no quarrels."

"Only because Helena kept her temper when you mislaid yours; like the day when you took her place, with incredibly ill manners, at breakfast, and the other day when you thrust your way unasked, and with that moron, into Daisyhill."

"I was not unasked," she cried. "I can read an invitation-card as well as you can. I waited for you to tell me, civilly, that we were all going, and then having watched you go off with Helena, as if I did not exist, I did what any woman of spirit would have done, and made my own arrangements."

"Woman of spirit! You have the spirit of a fishwife. Do not forget your origins, my dear wife."

"And do not forget—" she was near tears—"that without them you would still be a pauper, borrowing from Nigel. Have you paid him back what you owed him yet? Is that why he can buy Withenshaws?"

"Keep to your own affairs and leave me to mine," he answered coldly, and picked up a newspaper which had come, immuring himself behind it. She went to the window and looked out at the day; it was raining. Perhaps Belinda and the governess would enjoy it if she had the child come to the studio to play with the clay. Belinda was very neat in her handling; her queer little hands, with their short, almost useless thumbs, patted and stroked until she had made a mud-pie, and Sara showed her how to pinch it round the edges. It gave the governess too, poor soul, an hour off duty. She was a pallid creature, who looked as if she could do with a good walk.

She went up to the schoolroom and asked. Miss Bartlett stood up, made a little fussy movement with her thin hands and said, apologetically, "Lady Helena does not wish Belinda to go to the studio any more. She—she says it makes her clothes dirty. I am sorry about it, madam, for the child enjoyed it, and it was wonderful to see her *make* something. But it was not my place to say anything. I am truly sorry."

Belinda raised her head and beamed at Sara; none of the talk had touched her. She could only follow single words, or perhaps simple phrases. Sara bent and kissed her. "Writing?" she said, for there were hieroglyphics on the slate. Belinda nodded vigorously. Sara smiled, touched Miss Bartlett on the arm—it had not been her fault, of course not—and made her way downstairs alone. Once in the studio she unwrapped, not a lump of clay but a piece of beech wood, partly carved. She had already started on a likeness, from memory, of Helena. Now would be the time to let the spleen work itself out in the chisels and carve in that quality of evil which kept itself so subtly. She worked on, knowing it was better for her at the moment than lifting heavy weights of clay. That, in fact, was the reason why she had started the carving, at which she could sit if she chose. Despite Francis' unkindness to her she wanted his child to be born healthy, and did everything she could in the way of feeding herself carefully, and lacing not too tightly. By now she was beginning to thicken.

The features began to emerge from the wood. Sara took rough sandpaper and smoothed the high-boned cheeks, the long muscles of the neck. Then she set to work on the knot of hair at the back. That was less personal. But . . . Nigel to go! They would visit, doubtless, and the visits would be returned, but it would never be the same again.

Withenshaws was a grey house built thirty years before, with high gables. It was not beautiful but its gardens had been laid out formally, and would be pleasant to look upon. Nigel took Francis and Sara to see over the rooms; Helena would not come. The rain, which had continued for some days, had stopped, leaving everything fresh and green, the grass much overgrown. Shafts of sunlight slanted in at the uncurtained windows, showing the new wood of the floors; downstairs, there was a little ballroom with polished parquet. "You will become the hub of society," said Sara demurely, when Francis was out of hearing examining the window-sashes. "These are convenient, but not, I think, as pleasant as the small diamond panes at Ae," he said. "No," said Sara determinedly. "We would not want to change those." She turned to Nigel. "You and Helena will make it a very pleasant house, and it is not too far from us—how far?"

"About five miles."

It was Nigel who answered, because Francis was still too angry with her for being the cause of the move. If he is never going to speak to me again, she thought, we are going to have a merry time at Ae. She knew that he could bury himself in his books and papers, and even exert himself to oversee the estate with the factor; she would only see him at meals, in the presence of servants. She felt miserably uncertain suddenly. What would her life be like from now on? Admittedly there would be the child . . .

"Nigel, would you leave Belinda and the governess with us for a little while?"

She should have asked Francis first; he scowled, but Nigel turned to her with relief. "How kind that is of you!" he said. "She will be strange here . . . she has her own little corners at Ae . . . will it inconvenience you, Francis?"

"I shall never see her," replied Francis shortly, and added that as it would soon grow dark they had best go back.

So she had Belinda's company for a little, at any rate.

Helena persisted in her refusal to have anything to do with Withenshaws. "You bought it for Sara's sake," she said, and yawned. "Sara may help you furnish it."

So Sara helped him; being driven over by him every day in the phaeton, helping him take measurements or, often, going through decorators' books to choose wallpaper, curtains and carpets. She would have enjoyed it and his company but for one nagging thought; she is doing this on purpose, so that when he sits with her in the rooms I helped him furnish, he will remember me.

It was late autumn now and the trees about Withenshaws and Ae shed leaves, brown, red and yellow, causing the wheels of the phaeton to crunch with the noise small boys make shuffling crisp leaves in the park. The decorators had come and gone; they had chosen white mostly, because it lightened the rather heavy style of the house. It would be commented on, because others did not yet go beyond brown or, sometimes, green. "It improves it," said Sara. She was standing in the hallway that gave on to the little ballroom, which they were to drape with curtains of pale blue. Nigel was standing close to her; he took her hand.

"If only you were to come here with me, and not *her*—"

She had not the heart to draw away her hand; it tightened about his. "Surely you loved her when you married her," she said gently. "It cannot all have gone."

"All; there is nothing left. I can admire her beauty, as one might do a statue; I can listen to the compliments I receive on my beautiful wife from strangers. Friends know me too well to say such things, and perhaps that is why, over the years, I have made few friends."

"Francis is your friend, I think."

"You think?" He smiled at her. "Poor Sara, you are as wretched in your marriage as I in mine. Why do not we divorce? We would be outcasts, it is true, but would you not be outcast with me? Does what I read in your eyes mean nothing?"

She took her free hand and placed it on her abdomen. "There is *this*—his child and mine. I could not leave it to be brought up by him, any more than, though it is interference in me, I can leave Belinda to Helena. I love her, you see, and I shall love this baby even though—" She bit her lip. He turned away, frowning.

"So that it will be a great many years before I can hope to call you my own. Well, I will wait; give me hope, and I will wait."

"That would not be fair to you; you have enough to endure. Does it not trouble you, now, to think of Helena and Francis together?"

"Not a jot. Helena is made of ice, and even if I thought she were committing adultery with Francis—which I know she is not, her spell over him lies in her very coldness, which he mistakes for virtue—even if I thought that, it would not move me."

"Poor Nigel," she said sadly.

"And poor Sara. But we can comfort one another, five miles apart. I would not have made it a greater distance."

"And you will come to visit us?"

"Assuredly."

Other visitors came, as autumn gave way to winter; one day a couple of sisters, old maids, came in a new open carriage. Sara cried out with delight when she saw it, to the sisters' justifiable pride; they were swathed in veils, which they unwound for tea. They had been made acquainted with Sara already, at the famous *fête champêtre*; more and more she encouraged herself for having broken the traces and gone, and she would do that kind of thing again, despite Francis and his threats.

He came in just as the sisters were departing, displayed interest in the carriage, and stood with Sara to watch the departure. The veiled sisters waved farewell, and Sara joyously replied; they had promised her a drive in it, once the birth was over. When they had gone Francis' momentary interest faded, and he went to the hearth and kicked at the logs.

"It shows the state we are in, to have to be entertained by two old beldames who choose to call," he said.

"They were charming. One of them plays the viola."

"What good in hell is that to me?" he said. "What I need is talk, familiar chat, none of your damned dinner-parties. Get that governess woman to join us at dinner tonight; we'll see if she has a tongue in her head."

Sara rather doubted it; Miss Bartlett was a timid soul, much more likely to irritate Francis than amuse him. However, she promised to ask. Miss Bartlett flushed scarlet, professed herself delighted, and thanked everyone profusely. Sara left feeling a trifle guilty; she herself might have taken some note of the poor young woman before. The life of a governess was known to be hard; no doubt Miss Bartlett's place was devoid of the torments some children imposed, but she hardly ever saw anyone but Belinda.

That night she appeared in a maroon dress made of some shiny material, and had looped her hair loosely round her face and stuck a paste ornament in it. Sara preferred her neat daily appearance, but said nothing. She was beginning to be troubled by a headache, and was glad someone was there to talk to Francis; their customary silence would have beaten like waves across her brain. Francis, on the other hand, seemed to be in good spirits; he chaffed the governess, and seemed to take pleasure in shocking her a little. He asked her about her last place; he asked her about her future plans; he was the perfect host, incessantly plying her with wine. Poor Miss Bartlett's replies became confused and the paste ornament fell sideways on her head, giving her a giddy look. Her cheeks were bright with the wine. I cannot endure any more of this, thought Sara; I shall go to bed, and they may do as they choose about the port and coffee.

"My head aches very badly," she said when she might. "I think that if you will both excuse me, I will go to bed now. It should be better in the morning."

Francis almost leaped to the door to open it for her to go out; as she passed she gave him a direct look. He was unsmiling, but his eyes held devils. Am I right to go, and leave them alone? she thought. But she could not turn back now without looking foolish. She gathered her skirts and went upstairs.

"Ye'll be right as rain in the mornin'," Biddy assured her. "It's the state of things."

"A little more wine," said Francis persuasively. Miss Bartlett made a vague gesture of negation. "No?" he said, regretfully. Then "I have something which will just set you up; it takes away the effects of the wine; I always take a glass myself before going to bed. You will share one with me?"

"Oh—I thank you, but I—"

"That is splendid," he said, and went to the sideboard, where the brandy stood. He poured a glass for himself and one for her. "The trick is to take it in one gulp," he said, and watched her obey him. Almost instantly, Miss Bartlett collapsed in a heap on the table, breathing stertorously, the empty glass still in her hand. Francis smiled, removed it, and carried the unconscious woman to where, in a corner, a chaise-longue lay which matched her dress: it had gilt feet. At that moment the servant's face appeared round the door, waiting to clear up. "Do not come back for another half-hour," said Francis clearly; in fact he was somewhat surprised at his clarity, as he had been drinking a good deal during the day. He began to unfasten Miss Bartlett's bodice, and then to take down her drawers.

Much later—it was already morning—Miss Bartlett awoke in an unfamiliar bed. It was larger than her own, and the sheets were much rumpled. She brought her hands up to her breasts; they were naked. Where were her clothes? What had happened to—oh, her head! It was like red-hot irons; she lay down again, a prey now to both pain and shame. Things had taken place during that night she could hardly, but just, remember; things one's mama had always warned one about; somewhere among it all, a great unexpected surge of pleasure. To have felt *that* was worst of all. What would become of her? Oh, her head, her head! Her clothes, her clothes! How could she even get out of this room without them? What was she to do? What time was it? If she met anyone, she would die of shame. It had all begun—or ended—with that drink. How right they were who said drink was evil! She would never touch a drop again.

She crawled out of bed and, finding no clothes at all, concluded that . . . that *he* must have taken them away. Did that mean he would come back? Never, never could she endure it; she could not look him in the face again. And yet, she wanted to.

In the end she gathered her courage to her and found a bell-pull, jerked it, got quickly back into bed, and waited. It was answered by, of all people, Mrs Padstow. A glance at that turkey-cock face almost unmanned Miss Bartlett, but she summoned strength to say, in an even voice, "May I see Mrs Atherstone, please? She knows I am not feeling very well; please fetch her."

Mrs Padstow answered neither yea nor nay, but went out, closing the door, and to Miss Bartlett's infinite relief, Sara came. The poor governess burst into tears. "I didn't know what happened, ma'am," she wailed. "If I'd known, I'd never have touched the wine—or the other—it was that that finished me. I fainted with it, and the next thing I know I'm here, with all my clothes gone." She began to weep and sob; Sara put an arm round the bare shoulders.

"I should not have left you with him," she said. "It was my fault, not yours. Stay here, and first of all I will bring something to cure your head, and then I will bring some clothes. We will say nothing about all this to anybody." All the same, she was thinking, if she has a baby she will never get another situation.

Later, with Miss Bartlett cosseted, dressed, and led back to her own room—Sara took Belinda away for the day, dragging a toy by the hand—later, Sara went to look for her husband. She instructed Belinda to wait on the window-seat in the passage, to play with her toy and not to move for anybody. Then she marched into the library. Francis was there, legs stretched before him while his head drooped in a drowsy way. I'll wake him up, she thought.

"You are the lowest creature alive," she said clearly.

He raised his head; his eyes were bloodshot. "Am I, fishwife? Who says I may not do as I choose in my own house, eh? You found the wretched governess."

"And found her some clothes, which you had kindly removed from the room. She is resting now, but in a very bad state, poor thing. I am going to send her to Nigel and Helena for her own sake, with the child. This cannot happen again."

"Can happen tonight . . . tomorrow . . . over thirty, though." He smiled hazily, as though the fumes of brandy still mounted in his own brain. "Can you think of other people for a little while?" said Sara. "Have you ever done so in your life? That poor woman, who has her living to earn and must have references for it, may be with child by you. Are you going to support her and the child? Or is it only another pastime to you?"

"Good pastime . . . begettin'. How do you feel?" His glance roved insultingly over her, as it had on their wedding night.

"Are you going to support her—if that happens? Have you the innate decency to do that?"

"No need, no need. Marry her off to some farmer. Marry her to Runcatch. He'll lick her into shape, for a consideration."

"You have no heart in you at all, and I despise you more than I have ever done anyone in all my life. If it were not for the coming child I would leave you, but you are not fit to look after one. You—"

"And take refuge with Nigel, and send Helena back to me? That would suit everyone. No more visits from old ladies in veils for you, though. Your repu—reputation would be—trampled upon, like I trampled that wench last night. Lord, I'd lay twenty to one I remember more of it than she does. It wasn't time wasted, ha, ha!"

Sara went to him and gave him a ringing slap across the ear. Then she walked out of the room. As she did so she heard him shout, "If it were not for the child coming, who matters to me, you'd get that back with interest, you two-faced bitch! Just wait till you're free of it and I can get at your hide! Just wait till then!"

It was at that point, although it must have been latent in her mind, that Sara resolved to go with Miss Bartlett, Belinda and Biddy to Withenshaws and ask Nigel and Helena to grant them all four hospitality. The weather had grown very cold; but they would wrap up well, and take warm clothing with them; and in any case it was only a few miles. Sara gave orders for Runcatch to harness up the larger carriage; he could return with it when they were safe at Withenshaws.

Unfortunately Nigel was not at home. Helena received Sara, while the rest huddled with their hastily collected bundles in the hall. Helena was sitting alone before a log fire, sipping tea. "Do join me," she said languidly; she had not risen. The firelight flickered comfortably on the heavy Georgian silver; on a plate were buttered crumpets and little cakes. The room had already taken on some of Helena's personality; ornaments and kickshaws she had brought to Ae on her marriage now embellished the little tables, glass-fronted cupboards and mantel.

It was impossible not to explain why they were here, impossible not to betray the story of poor Miss Bartlett. To Sara's distaste Helena gave a harsh trill of laughter. "Well, at any rate she has had her *nuit d'amour*," she said, biting a crumpet. "How very bored Francis must have been to do such a thing! If I had been there, it would not have happened."

Sara ignored the supreme egoism of the latter statement. "But you were *not* there, and it *did* happen," she said firmly. "May we crave your hospitality at least in the meantime? It would not do for them to meet again, and I am beginning to be afraid of having dinner with Francis alone." She hated to admit the last; it was a measure, no doubt, of her own failure to interest her husband; but Helena must be lured into letting them stay.

"By all means stay here, if you wish it," said Helena languidly. She raised a white beringed hand to pull at the embroidered bell-cord. When the maid came she said,

"Take away these things. Then tell Mrs Paige that Mrs Atherstone will occupy the beige room, Miss Bartlett and Miss Belinda the blue, and—er—Biddy—it is Biddy, is it not?—will be found suitable occupation in the servants' quarters. That will be all. Oh, and you might take a collation up to the blue room. I daresay they are hungry after their journey."

"That is kind of you," said Sara warmly. Perhaps she had misjudged Helena a little. Yet later, changing for dinner in her beige-hung bedroom, she wished that Nigel had been present; now Helena would be first with her version of the affair, and somehow make them all seem ridiculous, in especial the poor governess. Perhaps we *are* ridiculous, she admitted to herself, as Biddy pinned up her hair.

"You have met friends downstairs?" she asked the maid, who nodded with her mouth full of hairpins. When she was free of them she answered "Oh, ay. Them and me's known each other from the comin's and goin's long since; they'd no need to ask me why we were here at all."

"Biddy, if you know, please do not tell them."

"I will not."

Sara knew Biddy's sharp eyes missed very little, but that she was trustworthy and would not make a laughing-stock of poor Miss Bartlett. What that poor woman's fate would be Sara could not yet imagine. If she were pregnant, one would give help—Francis' cure was a brutal one—and if she were not, it might be wiser to let her seek another place well removed from here, where there would be no gossip. Some of the servants at Ae must have seen or heard something of what had taken place last night. What it came to—Sara stared at her own reflection in the mirror, seeing a comely enough young woman despite her advanced pregnancy—what it really came to was that Miss Bartlett must never return to Ae. In that case, who would look after Belinda? In the ordinary way it was time her parents took her, but the situation was not ordinary, and Belinda would be unhappy in unfamiliar surroundings with no one she knew.

Well, she herself could do no more about it meantime; she was very tired, and it was with a great measure of relief that she heard the sounds of Nigel's return. Even if she had no chance to get in a word on the matter, she felt safer when he was there.

"Sara! What a delightful surprise!" he exclaimed when she entered the drawing-room. "Helena tells me you have come to stay for a little. That will be pleasant; it is time Withenshaws was used for guests, if I may call you so; in fact, you're the family."

She found herself unable to stop looking into his eyes; did he know why they were here, or not? Presently he gave a little nod, when Helena's head was turned away for a second; Sara felt a great burden lifted from her heart. Now, even if Francis came seeking her—which at this hour was hardly likely—she would have a champion in Nigel. She let him lead her in to dinner feeling much comforted. The three of them made pleasant talk; how different it was from last night! Miss Bartlett, no doubt, was having supper in her room. It was understandable that she did not want to face the company.

Sara passed a dreamless night, and in the morning, at breakfast, she and Nigel were the only ones present. He launched forth into the subject at once, as they might be interrupted at any moment. "I am going over to see Frank today, to make him behave sensibly over all this," he said.

"He is often like a small boy, who torments anyone he has to deal with."

"This is rather more than the antics of a small boy. Nigel, I am very much afraid for the future. I cannot talk to him, you see. When we are alone we sit and eat our food and drink our wine, and that is all. He will not think of me as anything but the working-class wife pressed upon him by Uncle Nicholas."

"He will think differently when I have done with him," said Nigel, his mouth grim. "You cannot continue as unhappy as you have been, nor can unprotected women in his house go in fear of him. He has behaved like a scoundrel, and—"

Sara had heard Helena's soft footfall. "I think that it is going to snow," she said, as beyond the window a few tiny flakes could be seen. "What a good thing we got here in time! It will make the roads slippery. Nigel, do you think you ought to ride over today? You might meet with an accident."

"Cloud is reliable," he answered, "and I must certainly ride to Ae."

The weather continued very cold, and there were puddles of ice in the ruts of the roads; there had been one or two small flurries of snow. But the ice continued implacably; and as the days passed there were hopes expressed that the ponds might freeze. The lake at Daisyhill was famous for its skating facilities and for the hospitality of Sir Charles, who allowed everyone, squires, farmers, labourers, everyone who owned a pair of skates, to take advantage of it and afterwards, had a trestle table set up with mulled wine for everybody.

Sara thought of it all wistfully; she had been a good skater, for Dad had taught her; but looking down at her size thought it would not be possible for her to try. Helena, to whom she mentioned it, laughed. "As long as you can keep upright you are in no danger," she said. "Nigel will give you his arm. As for Francis, if I thought he was going to be present—" she broke off, as if in confusion.

"Yes?" said Sara calmly. There had been not a word from Francis since the day Nigel returned, grim-lipped, from his lecture to him. Helena put up a hand as if to smooth her hair, which was perfectly in order.

"It is only that he takes me out in the toboggan," she said. "You might like it too."

"No, I will skate if I go at all," said Sara firmly.

The ice held, and towards the end of the week they all set off for Daisyhill, travelling early before the crowds would be free from their farm-work. Francis had arrived before them, and though he said no word to Nigel or Sara he bowed to Helena and said, "I have brought the sledge. Will you allow me to guide you?"

Sara said nothing, but let Nigel strap on her skates; there had luckily been several pairs of these, kept oiled and ready, at Withenshaws, and even a child's pair with double blades for Belinda. The little girl was jumping up and down with excitement, so that Sara had to hold her while Nigel put on her skates; she had never been on the ice before, and they planned to take her between them, slowly at first, to teach her to balance. Once over the edge, her confidence increased; soon she was skimming along between them, but rather dragging on them than moving of her own will.

"Try to do it as if you were walking, darling," Sara said. "A long long walk."

But that did not do, and presently Nigel said he would take his daughter out to the centre and, keeping nearby always, make her go back to Sara. The double skates were absolutely safe, and even if she did take a tumble she was robust enough. The queer little face was rosy inside its fur hood. Further off on the lake, Helena, glorious in white fox, was being spun round the ice in her toboggan by Francis.

"Would you like a little freedom?" said Nigel. "I will divert her while you skate. He watched Sara sway out to the centre of the ice, balancing well; she tried figures of eight and figures of three; she was happy, and evidently in her element. He took his eyes off her, and briefly, in the intervals of watching his daughter, looked for Francis and Helena. They were coming nearer.

"Belinda, come to me!" called Helena suddenly as they came into the part occupied by Sara. The sledge moved rapidly with Francis' thrusting strokes behind it. Before Nigel could stop her Belinda had blundered out on to the ice, and collided with Sara's figure which at that moment was precariously balanced on the turn of the three.

No one could be precisely sure what happened. They saw her fall; and a skater cannot fall forwards, so she landed, twisted, on her side and back. Nigel, swifter than thought, was by her; he knelt down and took her in his arms. "Sara," he whispered. "Sara." The pair in the toboggan had drawn close; Belinda had begun to roar and wail; he heard Sara say, in a low voice, "Something is . . . wrong, Nigel. Take me home."

He picked her up and skated with her to the edge, cursing the necessity of removing his skates before he could walk to the carriage. It was quickly done, and by now Francis and Helena had joined them, the latter, unusually, leading Belinda by the hand. They got Sara on to the seat of the carriage and let her lie there, her face turned away from them, white as the dead. If only there had been brandy,

Nigel thought; even, if Daisyhill had been appreciably nearer, they could have taken her there. But the park was immense, and it was best to get her back to Withenshaws. The carriage drove carefully, gently; but by the time they got home Sara's child was born and lying among her skirts. It was dead. It would have been a boy.

"And what business had she skating at all in her condition, with the child due in a matter of weeks? All this waiting for nothing, and now—"

"You will contain your tongue," said Nigel furiously. "If you had looked to what you were doing better she would have had no cause to fall. When did Helena ever call out to Belinda in her life before? Anyone would think—"

"Do not dare blame Helena," said Francis between his teeth. "Why, for two pins I'd take my wife out of here back to where she should be by rights—at Ae—"

"And kill her. That is what you would like to do, I do not doubt."

"How is she?" demanded Helena coolly.

"She weeps constantly. If it were not for that, and if she would even take milk, she would grow better. But like you, Francis, she regards the loss of the child as her fault, and will take no comfort from anyone." Biddy, he did not add, had sat by her mistress day and night. "And who was the culprit, if not Sara?" said Francis smoothly.

"Yourself. You and Helena. I say it to your faces. You should have stayed away from where we were, and you, you damned woman, had some devil's plan in you when you called to Belinda just *there*, where Sara was skating."

Helena rose. "I will not stay to be insulted. I shall go to my room."

"You may go to hell for all I care. I wonder what your soul

looks like, Helena? I have often wondered."

Francis interposed. "If you speak to Helena in that manner again in my hearing, I shall knock you down."

"And what about the way you talk to *your* wife, out of our hearing? That would not stand up to witnesses, I think."

Helena had gone to the door. Francis hastened to open it for her, and said a few words in a low voice.

"What did you say to her?" demanded Nigel sharply on his return. Francis smiled.

"Something that concerns a third person, not you or yours, my dear Nigel. For Sara is yours, is she not?"

"You insult her without need. At present she is very ill and may even die. You have misused her shockingly to have driven her here at all, and I say the blame of losing your son is your own."

He looked directly into the other's eyes, and turned, going out by the opposite door.

Sara stepped into the carriage, still with a feeling of weakness about the knees, following the days of weeping, the weeks of convalescence. Biddy had been her nurse, and no one could have been better; as she said, she'd seen her own mother have seven and lose three. It made one feel less solitary, less important; although certain things still had power to surprise her, such as the news that, some time ago, Miss Bartlett had taken Belinda back with her to Ae. If Miss Bartlett was not afraid, neither need she be. Nigel had remonstrated with her, saying that she would be unprotected, and must look after herself for longer, much longer.

Helena had said nothing. And Sara's own conscience told her to go.

She felt the coach drive off, waved to them all on the steps of Withenshaws, then turned her eyes on the road to Ae; she had preferred to take it alone. Francis was apprised of her coming, but had not driven over to fetch her. That might mean much or little; she would not know till she saw him again, the man she had married.

They came to the forest road and she saw the firs rearing to the sky, and then, on the sudden turning, Ae with its few planted deciduous trees, bare as skeletons for winter. They drove to the door and she dismounted, Biddy following with her gear. Mrs Padstow was at the door to greet her; it was like old times. "Where is Mr Francis?" she asked, looking full into the woman's high-coloured face. Its eyes were less impersonal than usual. "He's in the library, madam," the woman said, adding unexpectedly "We are all glad to see you back, madam, and hope that you will soon be well again."

"Thank you," she said, and without removing her outdoor things went straight to the library. Francis was sitting there, in his favourite chair. He allowed her the courtesy of rising.

There was a silence. Then she said what she had planned to say. "Francis, I know this has been my fault as much as yours. Cannot we start again? You would not have killed our little baby; I know that. I was so sad after I lost it that—that I could not think clearly, and then day after day as I lay in bed I thought 'What am I here for?' and I remembered that I had promised certain things to you in our marriage vows. If I can, I will give you another son. But it must be a contented pregnancy, with no alarums. Do you think we can contrive it, between us?" She smiled as well as her pale lips could, and approached the fire.

"Sit down," said Francis. "Yes, it was—my fault—as

much as yours. That I will admit. I think this marriage should never have been. I think Uncle Nick was to blame. If there had been the money, and I'd married Helena, I'd have been a different sort of fellow. As it is—"

"But we *are* married, and so are Helena and Nigel. I remember you said something—"

"About your belonging to Nigel?"

"I have never been unfaithful to you, Francis."

"Nor I to you—except with Miss Whatsername. As to that, there is news for you. The lady is married."

"Married? But—"

"To Runcatch. He was willing to take her for fifty guineas, so I paid it, and that episode is closed. Belinda you see, was noisy lacking her. She must stay."

She was horrified. "But *Runcatch*—half a gipsy—"

"Oh, they've settled down. They live over the stables, and Belinda runs about there and in the apple-loft. I asked Helena's approval before arranging it, and she thought it excellent."

"But—a marriage—what clergyman married them?" She still could not see genteel Miss Bartlett in the gipsy's bed.

"Oh, the Reverend Samuel," said Francis, grinning. "He owes me the living, so he cannot refuse my requests."

"The poor soul—the poor frightened soul—"

"Oh, she's taken to it better than you might imagine. You spoke of our starting again. Well, I'm willing; but don't let the past come between us any more."

"I promise," she said.

If she had known, the wedding night of Mr and Mrs Runcatch had been less calm than outward appearances would admit. The trembling woman had climbed the loft stairs at last, to find a neat enough little place to live; a cooking-stove, kept shining and black; two chairs and a table; a daguerreotype of Runcatch's relations, who looked a villainous lot on a smoky heath; and the bed. The bed was made of iron and covered with a patchwork quilt. She found herself wondering idly who had done the patchwork; it was well done, if worn.

"Who—" she began, as Runcatch came up behind her. Outside it was beginning to be dark; they would not go down again.

"Can ya fry bacon?" She murmured that she would try, but her experience as a cook was very small. "Ya'll learn," he said. "I'll do it the night." He broke two eggs and fried them with the bacon, and set them down on two chipped plates with hunks of bread. She felt that she could not eat, and only crumbled a little of the bread while the eggs congealed.

"That's the last time ya waste good food," he said, and took her plate and cleaned it up himself. He jerked his head to where she might find water and there was also a kettle, steaming on the stove. "Ya fills the kettle in't mornin', see? That kettle do have to be hot all the day. And ya sees to the fire. There's wood in the stable back, and coal I'll bring. And this place needs keepin' clean as a whistle, way it is now."

"I will try," she said in a faint voice.

"And there's another thing. You strip now; strip naked."

"Why, why, I—I never have—"

"Ya has, and that's why I'm goin' to teach ya a lesson. I'm half of me Romany and we like our women chaste. One lambasting'll do for this time, and after that ya keep your legs closed to any man except me. Strip, I say."

She obeyed him, trembling like a leaf, her narrow white body at last standing defenceless in the light of the fire. Runcatch went to the wall where his razor-strop hung. "Bend over the bed there," he told her.

"Please—"

"Bend over, or it'll be the worse for ya. This is just to keep mind, like."

She bent over; was this herself, Mary Bartlett, the prim and correct, who had always had genteel references? She felt the strop cut a great swathe through the air and land stinging on her flesh; his arm raised itself again and again, while the sharp double flick of the strop bruised, whipped, lacerated buttocks, shoulders, waist, thighs. She could hear his breath coming thick with the effort of beating her; by the end of it her body was all one pain, and tears ran down her face.

"Get on the bed now," he said, his voice still thick. She dared not disobey; she laid herself down, while he stripped himself of everything except underpants and vest, in which he slept. Then he flung himself on top of her. He entered her sharply, and the bed began to shake; downstairs, the stable lads saw the quivering ceiling and winked.

"They're at it," said one.

"Ay."

Nobody made any more remarks. The former Miss Bartlett had taken a step down into the servant class, and henceforth would be one of them.

A letter came from Aunt Beatie for Sara, which was not too usual an occurrence; Sara was not a good correspondent and her aunt had too much else to do. But she had been grieved over the loss of the baby. *You must guard your own health, for they say it takes quite a little time to recover from such accidents. I pray that you have better fortune on the next occasion.*

We do very little here but baking, gardening, visiting; I am suffering no little from the Rheumatics, so will rest my hand now and end by sending you my affectionate good wishes.

Your devoted aunt,
Beatrice Wollaston.

Sara put the letter aside; it might have come from another world, another life. She could not even recall Aunt Beatie's features clearly. Ae was her life now, not a doubt of it; and could not be changed by things like the sight of Mary Runcatch carrying a pail of slops across the yard, her apron soiled and her eyes reddened. Sara had wanted to go to her, to offer sympathy, but that would be an insult; or help, but what help was there? As the servants themselves would say, she had made her bed and she must lie on it. Yet it had not been her fault that Francis had taken her first . . .

Sara closed her eyes for moments, shutting out the day. Francis had taken her own offer of reconciliation literally, and she was pregnant again, too soon for her health, as Aunt Beatie would put it. She would live quietly and eat well, and give everything she had to the fashioning of this baby; she would not even lift or throw clay for fear of loosening the embryo. Sometimes she would wander into the little studio, seeing the air still stirred by the light dust from the drying clay; rows of greenware of her own making, pots and vases and bowls, stood on the shelves; she would like to get them fired soon. She spoke of it once to the housekeeper, with whom she was on increasingly good terms; Mrs Padstow seemed to have accepted her at last in Helena's place, which was a triumph. Francis, she knew, still rode over to visit Helena and Nigel; she herself had not left the grounds since leaving her bed.

She had asked, hardly hoping for the information, if Mrs

Padstow knew of anyone who could build her a small wood-fired kiln. "It's made of bricks covered with turf," she said, "and shelves inside to fire the ware. It needs feeding for a long time with wood, and I'd pay anyone who would do that; it means sitting up all night." She smiled.

"Then we can maybe use the things you've made, madam. Lovely things, they are."

"Alas, no. They have to be glazed as well. Then they would hold water. But the second firing doesn't take as long."

"I daresay Runcatch'd build ye the kiln. He always says he can do anything, and I daresay it's true enough; he's clever with mending saddles, and that. If you would like it, madam, I could ask him."

Sara had put a hand to her throat; she did not want any more dealings with Runcatch than she need. But it was foolish not to take the opportunity; it was possible he really could make a kiln.

He came and stood before her, dour and uncommunicative as usual, but he listened with intelligence to the instructions she gave and took and studied a small piece of paper on which she had made sketches.

"I could make it," he said. "I used to see kilns when I was in the north, tradin' ponies. Sometimes I'd watch the white fired ware bein' unloaded and carted away. Ay, I can make a kiln."

"Very well. We will choose a good flat place, not too near the house because of the fumes, and not near trees; the kiln gets very hot."

"Ay." He would not speak further of it, and half doubtfully she let him go away, wondering if she would ever hear of the matter again. But now Francis drove himself wherever he wanted to go the coachman had more leisure. One day he came to Sara, looking no better pleased than before, to say the kiln was done.

"I will come and see it," said Sara. "I've kept away all this time, knowing it was best to leave you to do it your own way."

"It's a queer fadge for a woman," was all he would reply, but he led her to the little kiln, built carefully of loose bricks in the shape of a beehive, with a good chimney and a space beneath to feed in the wood. He had chopped and piled the latter nearby, also squares of dried turf to cover the firing. Sara was pleased, and turned impulsively to thank him.

"I must pay you what it's worth," she said. "What is your price?" He looked at her speculatively, then named a price which was far too high. Sara knew it, but paid him. Perhaps there was an unacknowledged notion somewhere in her mind that if he were pleased with the money, he would be kinder to Mary.

She would allow no one to pack the kiln but herself, and recruited a young groom named Bobby Dill to help her wheel the treasures in a barrow, having explained to him that they would flake or shatter at the slightest jolt. Bobby was careful, and the first consignment reached the kiln whole; she made him watch her while she took each piece carefully, placed it against the brick interior and then put another by it, using extra bricks for stands if necessary. "When they're fired, they will be hard, and won't break unless you drop them," she explained. "It doesn't matter if the touch one another during a biscuit firing. But when we come to the glazing, they'll need more space and it will take fewer."

He watched her arrange the ware with knowledge and skill, this quiet strange woman who they said wasn't too happy with the master, but was nevertheless his wife. He himself began to feel the excitement that comes at the prospect of a firing. When Sara had done packing she told him to take bricks and heavy turves and lay them in their place, and pack the lower space with the dry wood which would burn in an up-draught to the chimney.

Nigel and Francis came to see the start of the firing, with Belinda led by her father's hand; Helena had an engagement elsewhere. The match was placed among the dry wood and a tongue of flame grew, spread, and finally roared in an upward draught, causing red fire to be seen above the chimney. Bobby had undertaken to sit all night to fire it; Runcatch and Mary stood a little in the background, watching the kiln at work.

Sara stood up, and latched her arm in that of Francis. "Beer for everyone," she said, and laughed so that her white teeth showed in pleasure. Beer it was; for the grooms, for the Runcatches, anyone who had helped to provide cut wood or cart greenware or dig turves. The men cheered, and wished luck to the firing; Mrs Atherstone was a sport, there wouldn't have been beer in the old days.

Next day Bobby, dropping with sleep, let the fire out nine hours after it had been lit. His mistress had threatened him with every imaginable torment if he even took a peep, so he didn't; he yawned and went to bed. The fired ware cooled in its own time, and later Sara came and cautiously turned up the corner of a turf; there was no sound of cracking from within. Later still, she returned with a refreshed Bobby and took out the biscuit ware, still warm, from its embers. "We've made something," she said, and the look on her face was as near that of an angel as Bobby would ever see; it made him glad he'd helped with the firing, willing to help again whenever she needed him. "When do we glaze, mistress?" he asked, and she turned her smile on him and captured his heart.

"Whenever I have the glaze made up. It's made from whiting, and this time I'll just glaze the insides and then we can use the pots and things in the kitchen. It's exciting, isn't it, Bobby?"

Bobby nodded wordlessly, diverted by the harmless *ping* the pinkish ware took against a finger now that it had been fired. It was good to work for the mistress; himself, by now he'd as soon be a potter as a groom, although he loved horses.

Francis was lounging in a chair in the drawing-room at Withenshaws, while Helena sat with her back to him at the desk, finishing a letter. He was aware, as always in her company, of beauty and cool silence. The furnishings she had chosen for the new house were impeccable, of a shade between primroses and cream; they set off her gleaming hair, which today was twisted higher on her neck than usual, showing small unruly ringlets against the white flesh. She wore a striped morning-dress which would not have become most fair women; but the boldness of the design was muted by tiny flowers, embroidered with their leaves at intervals between the stripes. The elegant scratching of the nib on the expensive paper went on; somehow one knew that Helena would never emerge with a blot on her finger. Such thoughts did not occur to Francis, who was devoid of humour. If he had not been, how could he have worshipped for so many years a woman who would never be anything to him other than a friend? To gaze at Helena, he could have replied, would be reward enough. He found himself unable to forgive Nigel for causing that ugly lump of a child to be made in so fair a body, to have caused glorious Helena pain in the ridding of it. She never mentioned Belinda; it was as though she had cast her off at birth, as animals will sometimes do for no reason. But Helena had a reason. Francis congratulated himself afresh for having given the creature houseroom at Ae.

Helena sealed the letter and rose, bestowing a coveted smile on him. "We are good friends, Francis," she said. "Only a true friend would sit in companionable silence while I write invitation-acceptances."

"It is my pleasure to watch you," he said.

"Dear Francis," she replied vaguely. She sat down on the small gilt-legged sofa, arranging her skirts. It faced the south window, and a frown creased her white brow for an instant, then was gone. "I am forever at Nigel to uproot those dreary willows, drain the ground and put in an artificial pond," she said. "Waterfowl would be delightful, do you not agree?"

They discussed waterfowl. Presently Francis rose to take his leave. "I must go," he replied to her protests, "because a servant is taken in labour, and my wife troubles herself about it to a degree that may harm her if I am not present."

"Troubled over a servant?" Helena raised her fair brows. "They give birth like cattle. I trust Sara takes care of herself this time? So much depends on it."

"Eighty thousand pounds," said Francis grimly. "Uncle Nick must be enjoying his jest in the infernal regions."

"The money will be yours one day. Do not fret over it."

They parted, he bowing over her hand with the manners of another age. It was always so when he was alone with Helena, as though she were Marie Antoinette. The notion had not occurred to him, but he rode good-temperedly back to Ae in the heat of late summer, seeing the leaves almost ready to turn their colour, no longer true green. It was pleasant to be able to visit Helena whenever he wished, without trouble from Nigel or Sara.

After he had gone Helena did not let her smile fade; she had put in two needling sayings, which while Francis—dear Francis!—would not recognise them for what they were, would in the end disturb him; firstly the remark about invitations—there were few now at Ae, the county not having quite accepted Sara although some had visited her—and, secondly, the artificial lake. If he thought of it, and remembered her saying it, he would recall also the day Sara had lost him his heir by behaving foolishly on the ice at Daisyhill. The satisfaction of such victories was small, but kept him by her side, especially as—she shrugged—Sara herself seemed more greatly interested in clay and servants than in her own husband.

Sara, her own body heavy now, had in fact gone straight to Mary Runcatch when she heard she was in labour. She mounted the loft stairs carefully—one must not trip—to be met by Runcatch himself at the top. He stood barring her way. From the bed came small soft yelling sounds like an animal in pain.

"Let me go to her." But he would not move.

"There's no one goes to my woman except me. I'll see it born and all put right. We don't want strangers."

"Runcatch, I'm not a stranger; I knew Mary before you did."

"I'm lettin' no one in," he repeated, and the sounds of anguish from the bed increased; he did not turn his head. Sara could not see Mary from where she stood; the iron bedstead and the steam from the kettle on the stove prevented her. She was glad he had hot water. No doubt he could manage, but Mary—

"Let me know if you need anything, Mary, and I'll send it over," she called. A voice, thin with pain, replied "No—

no—it was kind—"

Runcatch shut the door in her face.

As she went down the ladder, flushed and troubled by the encounter—supposing the poor woman died for lack of care?—she heard sounds of laughter in the loft. She knew who it was; Belinda, among last year's apples. The child's face appeared at the entry as she passed by, laughing still. "Let me down," called Belinda. "Let me down, aunty. Ladder."

Sara found a groom and saw him hoist a ladder, and watched Belinda climb down, swift as a monkey. It struck her that the girl's clothes were badly put on; no doubt poor Mary Runcatch had other things to do than fasten buttons. "Come here, child, and I'll set you straight," Sara called.

Belinda came obediently, and Sara adjusted her clothes. How had she got them so disarranged by merely climbing up to the apple-loft? "Now you are neat and tidy again," she said, noting at that same time that Belinda had matured amazingly during the past months; she was no longer a child, but a woman. Yet her mind would always be a child's. It was a sad business.

"Francis, I'm worried about Mary Runcatch. She's in labour, and he won't let me in, or anyone. Would you go and ask, and take her some grapes? He won't refuse you. The poor woman may need a doctor, or certainly a midwife.

Runcatch is doing everything himself."

"You have to remember that he's half a Romany. They guard their rights very jealously. Still, I don't see why she shouldn't have some grapes. I'll see what I can do."

He took the wrapped package and went out, round by the stables, and up the loft stairs, knocking at the closed door. No one answered. Francis lifted the latch and went into the room. In the bed, snoring a trifle, Mary Runcatch slept. There was a bundle near her which was the baby. Francis laid the grapes by her bedside, bent over and lifted away the blanket from the baby's face; and beheld his own son.

There was no doubt about it; later, the resemblance would be less easy to see. But the light-brown curls, which would darken later, were his own, not Runcatch's; and he fancied he saw himself again in the tiny features and the shape of the hands. A feeling of extreme elation came to him. If only Sara bore a son also! If only—but the prospect was grotesque—he had married Mary himself, the money now would be his. But he knew very well Mary would not have satisfied him bodily unless he was drunk.

He went out of the room, closing the door carefully behind him. There was still no sign of Runcatch. If Sara asked questions, he could say truthfully that Mary was looked after; a low fire burned in the grate, and the kettle was ready; a jug of cold water had been placed by her bed. All signs of the birth, of blood, the rest, had been cleared away and probably burned in the fire. Runcatch could turn his hand to most things. He was a good man to have about.

A few yards away, in the apple-loft, Runcatch himself was copulating with Belinda. He had been doing it at intervals now for some months. The thin sour flesh of the Goy woman he had married did not satisfy him; he was not interested in Belinda's face or her wits, but in her plump pink, well-fed, sweet-smelling flesh, which he had exposed today as usual by rucking up her dress and taking down her drawers. Belinda cooed in ecstasy; she did not understand what it all meant except that it was pleasant. At first he'd only teased her, tickling her ribs, then when she laughed at that would come to him easily; he would thrust a hand up her groin, which was a beginning; the rest hadn't been difficult. She was an innocent, had been told nothing, understood nothing; and he himself had tried to be careful. He was elated today, and must keep watch on himself; the business of his wife's labour was over and soon, all things considered, she'd be available again; a child a year, that was what to give them when they had highfalutin' notions; it kept them in their place.

He smoothed Belinda's thigh with his thumb, and she writhed with pleasure, her tongue out. The faint smell of apples drifted to Runcatch. The loft was dry and well aired, and they'd kept all year without spot or mould. Afterwards, he'd give one to Belinda and leave her munching it; it served as an excuse for her presence in the loft, if anyone asked: so far, no one had done so.

In the last few days before labour began Sara felt a crying need to go down to the studio again and work; it was as if the child within her could not be born unless and until she declared herself a craftsman again. But she would adhere to her own promise of not lifting heavy weights. The idea had come to her to model a baby's head; not old enough to show upright on its neck, but a new baby, its head laid against the mother at an angle, its curved cheek and tiny ear showing. There was modelling clay in a bin, kept soft by constantly renewed wet cloths beneath the lid. She donned her potter's overall and began to work, building up the foundation with quick sure dabs of clay. When the head was started she made it hollow at first, intending later to stuff it with inflammable straw or paper; she had done this already, making little animals when there was clay left over from pots. It made the product lighter and burned to ash in the kiln if one left it an escape-hole. The escape-holes would be the baby's ear and mouth; already she was modelling the ear, delicate as a shell, the tiny convolutions exact in miniscule as she had seen them on many heads; one never knew what one stored away in one's mind's eye, and for what purpose. The infinitesimal dip of the temple, the rounding of the fragile skull, took time; everything must be right. She had stopped and was examining bins to find the one in which she kept straw, when Biddy appeared in the doorway. "Lord, madam, lunch is on the table, and the master says he won't wait."

"Tell him I will come," she said, and laughed and pulled the potter's slop over her head. Her pregnant body was made clear to her once more; she was no longer a worker in clay but the house's mistress. Biddy had scurried off with her message and Sara went and rinsed her hands, trying to erase the clay line which always appeared under her nails when dry; it irritated Francis.

She walked in late, and made her apology. "It was as well to start without me," she said, and took her place.

"Just as well, for the soup would have got cold." He asked what she had been doing, without any great interest; he was even unaware of the glow on her face, which always came when she had satisfied herself, working. "Oh," she said, "I was down in my old studio, modelling something, forgetting the time. It goes so quickly."

"Better out in the sun; it was one of the last good days we'll get."

"What did you do?"

"Went for a ride, as always; then I came back and walked about the place. The apple-trees are good this year."

"Did you see my garden?" She had, in the spring and summer, dug a little plot which she had planted with flowers. They were almost over now.

"A few marigolds," said Francis. "At Withenshaws they're planning a lake."

"We will have no lake here." She shut her eyes for instants, recalling the agony of last year. "I am sorry, Sara," said Francis. "I had forgotten."

They maintained courtesy towards one another, she thought; it was like a couple in a copy-book. After luncheon she returned to her modelling, for its walls were so thin that it would dry out quickly; she took the wet cloth off the little head and went to work, and soon forgot the episode of the pond. In any case one could let oneself get to a state when any word, any allusion, would hurt. She modelled on. The servants had instructions to say that she was not at home while working in the studio, and whether any visitors called or not she was unaware. Afterwards, looking at the little finished head, smoothing it here and there with a finger, she told herself that she should have been a hermit; a nun, except that she would not have obeyed the Mother Superior. An artist was a lonely person; Dad had been so, and had rejoiced in his loneliness; although he had loved her mother it had not destroyed him when she died.

She left the little head to dry out, its sleepy swollen lids like buds, its mouth like a rose; and went upstairs. She was not tired; but for the sake of her own pregnancy she went and put her feet up on the chaise-longue, flinging a shawl over them. She had a book to hand and started to read it. Francis came in at one point; they exchanged words, pleasant enough, and then he went out again.

During the next few days she was restless. It was not time to fire the head, although she would have liked to do so as it was fragile; it would disintegrate in the kiln if it were not thoroughly dry. She went to it often, and brooded over it; but oftener she went over Ae.

She would go to the rooms on the ground floor, that Helena had furnished tastefully; that had never troubled her. The gilt mirrors shone, so did the woodwork, every velvet surface was brushed and dusted, the paint and glass gleamed with care. Then she would climb to the upper floors and attics, with their smell of old dry wood and stored sunshine and the forgotten things she would find; crinoline-frames, a broken doll in a linen cap, a ruined harpsichord. One day Mrs Padstow, on her own thorough rounds, came on her. "Is there anything you would like moved, madam?" she asked courteously. In spite of her dislike of change she'd grown fond of this strange solitary girl who'd married Ae. She was no doormat, either, Mrs Sara; she knew what she liked and what she didn't like, and said so. Lady Helena had been different; earl's daughter or not, she'd never said a word of appreciation, not once. Withenshaws was welcome to her. Why the master rode so often over there was his own business, but for her own part she would have thought he'd find his happiness here, if he cared to look for it. He ought to be in the house anyhow, with the baby so near.

"I don't want anything moved, Mrs Padstow," said Sara, smiling a little. "I love to go all through this house exactly as it is, and admire things and touch them, even the brickwork of the walls. I don't think I spoil your polished wood with fingerprints."

"Never, madam; and it's nice to have it noticed. What would you like cook to make for tomorrow?"

"Steak pie with plenty of kidney, and a syllabub."

"And for dinner?"

"Oh . . . what do you think, Mrs Padstow?" Her mind had given out; she did not feel like discussing food. Mrs Padstow suggested a suitable menu and Sara agreed.

In the event, she was unable to be present at dinner; her labour began at four o'clock, a few days sooner than expected. Biddy put her to bed, with the comforting stone hot-water bottle Biddy still called a brick; and she lay looking out at the leaves making ready to fall. It was not so long since the terrible accident on the ice last year. She must forget that; and pray for Francis' son.

The last birth had been precipitate, a swift searing agony; this was longer, steady, rhythmic, fruitful; certainly the child lived. They had sent for a midwife Sara did not care for greatly; Helena had had her for the birth of Belinda. She was a smug woman with downcast eyes. "It's coming," she would say, "but not yet awhile. When it comes, bear down." Every so often she would come and feel Sara's stomach, and place the child; it was normal, she said; the head would come first. "After that there's nothin' to it. You bear down, and then leave it to me." She went back to the hearth; they had had to light a fire although the day was not too cold, to boil water. Sara felt the pains start again and bit her lips; she would not cry out in presence of this woman. "It's coming now, I think," she said.

"Bear down."

Did they never say anything else? Her whole body was pain; she could feel the child beginning to force its way out of her, even as the little clay model had, painlessly, done. Creation, birth . . .

"Bear down. The head shows now. It has dark hair."

It would be bound to, thought Sara. She bore down with all her power against the midwife's thrusting hand, placed to prevent a sudden birth which might injure the brain. At last her pains eased and she heard the woman say "It's born."

"Which is it?"

"A girl, a beautiful healthy little girl. I'll wash her and then bring her to you."

She must have floated back into half-sleep, half waking, because in a dream Francis was there, and he was angry. His eyes shone with fire like a devil's, and his mouth was hard. He hadn't looked at the baby, and she tried to humour him, to smile. "She's pretty," she coaxed him. "What shall we call her?"

"There is a name Meribah, which means waters of bitterness. We'll call her that."

Later, much later, she had awakened and had found the baby sleeping by her side; it looked large for a newborn girl, and its hair was curly and light brown. No doubt it had dried out to that colour. She was aware of trouble in her mind concerning it; something was wrong. Presently—it must in reality have been several hours—Helena came into the room, bent down and kissed her, leaving a scent behind her of verbena; smiling, she pulled aside the baby's shawl.

"He's a fine fellow," she said. "He looks like Francis."

Sara frowned a little. "She's a girl. Francis wants to call her Meribah."

"No, no; you have given him a fine son. Hasn't she, Mrs Upshaw?" The midwife was still in attendance, her eyes cast down to the carpet.

"Yes, a fine son," she said obediently. Sara felt madness overtake her; she sat up in the bed.

"But you said it was a girl, a beautiful healthy little girl . . . those were your words . . . ."

"You were dreaming, madam, imagining things. Look at the baby for yourself."

It is not my baby, thought Sara, half crazed. What had they done with her? She began to call aloud. "Where is she? Where is she? Where is my baby?"

"Calm yourself, my dear, and settle back on the pillows. It was a dream you had."

"You are a devil, and it was no dream. This child is not mine. Where is my child? Where is she?"

Runcatch and his wife sat in a cart, with Mary holding the new baby; they were driving off into the hills. Mary was subdued now, no spirit left in her; she would do anything her husband commanded without asking questions. There had not even been much curiosity in her when Mr Francis himself came, while she had been feeding her boy, given her husband money, put another baby into her arms, and gone away with hers. Runcatch would know what it was about. At his command, also, she had gathered together their few things and, still walking shakily, followed him down the loft stairs to where the cart waited with the pony ready in its traces. They turned out of the courtyard of Ae and made off through the forest, and Mary stared down at the different baby she now held; much smaller, it was, than her own, and newly born. Its hair was dark. She began to have a feeling for it, she who had thought she would never feel for anything or anyone again. They were going to Runcatch's people. He knew where to find them. She asked no questions. One took things as they came, that was all, and then he wouldn't beat her so often.

Francis had recovered from his first madness at the news. When he heard it he had gone down to Sara's studio, crushed the fragile head she had been making and kicked the fragments of clay and straw over the floor. Then he went to where Runcatch had built her a kiln; it was cold now, and gave him no hindrance as he kicked and destroyed the careful symmetry of the beehive shape, scattering the bricks and turves till all was flat, lying in rubble about the ground. It was at that point he had looked up and seen Runcatch watching him, expressionlessly, with his arms folded across his chest. The idea had come to him then; give Runcatch money and take his child, and get the other out of here, it didn't matter where or how soon. He had no memory of talking to Runcatch, or of saying the things he had to say. All he remembered was the exchange of gold coins, and going up to the midwife while Sara slept and seeing her also. Helena would do the rest. Helena knew how much he needed Uncle Nicholas' money. She'd visit Sara, convince her. If they all played their parts, Sara would believe them in the end. And the lawyer would never investigate. *Dear Mr Buckler, I am glad to say that my wife has today been delivered of a healthy son, in ratification*—that was a good word—*of the latter clause in my uncle's will. Perhaps you will set matters on foot at your early convenience. Your devoted servant, Francis Atherstone.*

"She can't go on like this. If she does, she'll lose her milk. There is nothing I can do to stop that. As it is, she won't feed the baby; I drew off some milk from her and fed it with a teat, and she nearly killed me. If I was you I'd get the doctor to her, to do what's needed; maybe a sedative would calm her, or maybe again he'll put the baby on some fancy food."

Francis frowned; he did not want a doctor or any other representative of law and order at the moment. He temporised. "If she is not better tomorrow, I will fetch him. Things may improve."

"I can go, then, sir?" The woman stood there, waiting to be paid. She had raised her eyes and he read contempt in them. He tried to ingratiate her. "Say nothing of all this, and here is an extra guinea," he said. "If you gossip, you know, you will do yourself harm."

"I'm not a gossip, sir, luckily. There's nobody that will spread any of this that I know of—except *her*. You won't quiet her."

The doctor was sent for on the following day; Francis talked to him and said that his wife had seemed crazed since the birth. Hoping that he had given a convincing picture of puerperal fever—he knew very little of its symptoms—he led the man to Sara's room, and was annoyed to find himself shut out. He lingered in the passage outside, waiting for news.

The doctor, who had come from Brede, let his cautious blue eyes rest on the patient. She was tossing and sobbing; the baby lay wailing in its cradle in a corner. His first instinct was to get the mother quietened and then the child fed. He approached the bed. Sara's green gaze, red-lidded, looked up at him.

"Are you the doctor?" she asked; her voice was hoarse

with weeping. Poor woman, he thought, she doesn't seem fevered; he put a hand on her brow and felt her pulse. She began to talk in a low voice. "Don't listen to them," she said. "I'm not crazy. Listen to me; don't give me a sedative. Go and examine that child, and see if you agree that it could not have been born yesterday."

"It may die tomorrow, unless it gets some food."

"I cannot—*cannot*—touch it. It isn't mine. They took mine away and brought it in. I know now where they brought it from. It is the coachman's child, or rather his wife's, and it happened to be a boy. My husband needed a son for his own concerns." A kind of loyalty, though she owed him little enough, stayed with her for Francis. Only let the doctor be a witness for her—one sane witness—and she'd wait till she could act. She was strong enough; it wouldn't need more than a day or two. But the anxiety for her own baby gnawed at her; where was she, what was happening to her, who was feeding her, Meribah, the waters of bitterness?

The doctor straightened from the cradle and came back to her bed and spoke in a low voice.

"You are right," he said. "I must speak carefully, because your husband is waiting outside the door. You must have enemies for this to have happened. For what it is worth, I give you my word that I will testify, even in a court of law, that this child is a week older than they said. Why, his eyes are open! He has, you know, a look of your husband."

"I know that. It is possible that he is my husband's child. But he is not *my* child. I will be good enough to him if they fetch me my daughter back."

"I can say nothing of that; it is not my concern. Get yourself well—I think you look better since talking to me—and meantime I will put the child on an artificial milk diet. If possible, I will persuade Mr Atherstone to employ a nurse to administer it. Does that help you?"

"It helps me greatly—I am so grateful—"

"Then be calm. It does no good to scream and fling yourself about the bed. Lie down and pretend to be sleeping, as though I had sedated you, when they come. Remember that you have my word to help you."

"And you do not think I am insane?"

He allowed a smile to lighten his normally austere face. "I think it possible that you are the only sane person at Ae. But do not tell them I said so."

She made herself wait for a long day, hoping that Nigel might come; but he did not. She pretended to be still drowsy with the drug they assumed had been given her, drank some milk and sherry whey, caused no trouble. But when they brought her the child Sara seemed fretful, and they took it into a further room where, she supposed, the nurse was looking after it; at least it was quiet. Poor child, she wished it no harm; but it was not hers.

That night she made herself stay awake, waiting till the stars should have begun to pale; they had been very bright beyond the window. She swung her legs down from the bed, still feeling weak; and made herself walk, slowly at first, then more strongly, to the cupboard where her clothes hung. She chose an easy-fitting dress of brown wool, and a caped coat to cover it; she found stockings and shoes, and tied a scarf about her head.

It was not too light when she stole downstairs. The best way lay through the studio and the back entry, and this she took, negotiating the stairs. A shock came to her as she saw the studio, still by starlight; the baby's head she had fashioned was gone, and fragments of sharp clay strewed the floor. An irrevocable sense of loss came to her. Francis, she knew, must have done this in his anger; did it mean she would never see her own baby again?

She left the studio, tears in her eyes, and fumbled for the latch that gave on to the yard. The windows of the Runcatch loft were dark and, although it was night, she knew that they had gone. She groped her way carefully past the stables, not to wake the grooms; then set out on the forest road. If it took her till morning to reach Nigel, she would bear it. Of all help she most desired his; of all presence, his. The longing for him seared her and made her forget her weakness; soon, she was striding along the path. Dawn broke, and made the going easier.

She walked on, she did not know for how long; it was still too early for anyone to have discovered her absence. Already she wondered if she had been foolish; a letter to Nigel would have brought him to her. But she had to see him alone.

The sky lightened, and the last pale planet faded; Venus herself, the sign of Mary Magdalen. The sun began to come up through the trees and banish the night-dew which had soaked Sara's shoes; the early scent of pine-needles came to her. A desire came also to sit down and rest among the trees; but she must not do that, it would give them time at Ae to find that she had gone, and to send out a search-party which would discover her quickly. Why did she fancy that with Nigel she would be safe? Yet she knew it; she might be Francis' wife, but she was Nigel's love. She was as clearly aware of it as if it had been written before her. He would help her; he would protect her, and find out about the child. What Helena's servants would have to say about her appearance at the door of Withenshaws unaccompanied, unkempt, and with no carriage, she did not know or care; it had only just occurred to her to think of them.

She walked on, but less valiantly now; weakness was beginning to overtake her again, and she knew that despite her resolve she would very soon have to sit down and rest, hiding herself among the moss and fallen branches. What poor things women were, always at the discrimination of men!

She would not be Francis' wife again. What he had done had made him loathsome to her.

She was making her way slowly, the dizziness like a ringing in her ears, until she realised that there were hoofbeats; they were coming out to look for her. She grasped her skirts, and half stepped, half fell into a green place, where she might be overlooked; late ferns still reared there, and she remembered noticing their shapes; fiddlehead, hart's tongue. She lay flat in fear, hiding her face and hands; there was not yet so much light that they would see her if she were careful not to expose her skin.

But the rider was coming the opposite way, from Withenshaws; going at a steady canter. It was Nigel. She scrambled up, and, flinging herself out on the path, screamed his name.

"Nigel!" The trees seemed to echo it round about; surely he could not have failed to hear, or was he turning round? She felt her knees give way suddenly; everything became blackness.

She wakened in his arms. He had put his cloak about her, still keeping it over his own shoulders so that the warmth of his body should penetrate hers. His face peered anxiously down at her; when she opened her eyes he said, relieved, "Sara! I—I thought you were dead."

"Not now." She was aware of nothing but utter contentment, here in his arms. His horse had strayed a little way off; they were back from the path, in a place something like the one she had selected; but not the same. "What are you doing out of bed?" he asked. "What has happened? What—"

"I was coming to you. I was hurt that you had not visited me. I needed you, and you did not come."

"I came every day—oh, not to the house. I would ride out like this, in the very early morning, but could not bear the sight of Ae, or the thought that, again, you had borne Francis' child."

Suddenly, rapidly, she told him what had happened. At the end of it she found herself breaking down into sobs. "And he destroyed the baby's head I'd made—out of clay—I was going to fire it—and he kicked the kiln to pieces. I think he's mad."

"You shall not go back to him," he said. Suddenly he lifted her in his arms, as though she had been light as a feather. "Were are we going?" she said, like a child.

"You are coming back with me to Withenshaws, straight to bed."

"But Helena—"

"Helena will do as I bid her. From now on your home is with me. You have endured enough."

She awoke to bright daylight shining between dimity curtains; the bed she lay in was as soft as down. For instants her mind circled in an attempt to remind herself of what had happened, where she was; then she remembered. She would have allowed herself to sink back into sleep again, but a neat little maid, in lace cap and apron and white cotton stockings, knocked at the door, came in, and laid a tray of light food by Sara's bed.

"The master says that if you feel like eating a bit, that's good, but if not to leave it," she said politely. Sara made herself swallow a glassful of milk and left the rest; despite her exertions at dawn she was not hungry. All anxiety, curiously, had left her; everything—even the ordering of food, evidently—was in the hands of "the master."

In fact, Nigel was no longer in the house, but driving back from Ae with a frozen Helena beside him. They had had words about her accompanying him that morning. She had been at her desk, as usual; he often wondered if it was an excuse for not confronting him directly.

"I cannot come with you to Ae," she said coldly. "I expect Lady Elham and her daughter for a morning-call."

"Then I will wait till they have come and gone, and you will accompany me then."

She twisted round in her chair; the action showed him at once the smallness of her waist, the perfection of her bosom, and the flush on her face. "Why do you always act so?" she asked him. "You are perfectly capable of talking with Francis lacking me."

His eyes had narrowed. "There wasn't any morning-call, was there, Helena?" he said softly. "You were going to wait till I was out of the house, then go up to Sara and either scare her or deceive her in some manner. I will not have her treated so; I would rather she need not see you at all, and for the present I myself will keep you from her, till she is rested. Also, as regards Ae, it may not have occurred to you that there is now no one left there to care for our daughter." Sara had told him the Runcatches had left, probably with her baby; and he had already set two good fellows of his own to try to find which way the half-gipsy family had taken. For this reason, he did not want to be too long away from Withenshaws; he had known it would be unnecessary to wait with Helena for non-existent guests.

"Our daughter!" pouted Helena. "Do not bring that monster here; I would be ashamed of showing her to anyone."

"Comfort yourself; she has not been shown to so very many at Ae. It is time I took her from Francis and got her a new governess, one who will understand her."

Helena gave her harsh laugh. "Understand? What is there to understand? She is an animal."

"Get your things, and say no more to me." He had had to exercise control to keep his hands from her. He had never punished her physically in any way; it would have been like beating a marble Aphrodite; but the day might come.

So they had reached Ae; Francis was waiting for them in the study. He did not seem in any great concern over the loss of Sara. The boy child was doing well on his new feed; that was all that mattered. If the lawyer called, he could say that Sara had been sent to Helena for a few days' rest; in fact, he had it in his mind that that was where she had probably gone. There was, therefore, no surprise on his face when he greeted the couple and saw Nigel's grim mouth.

"So Sara came to you. How very good of you to keep her, Helena. It was foolish of her to leave her bed."

"She had the best of reasons for leaving it, and this house. Her child had been taken from her and replaced by another. I do not know how most women would have behaved in the circumstances, but Sara seems to me to have acted most naturally."

Francis smiled. "But then, Nigel, you were always Sara's champion. I wonder what Helena has to say?"

Helena had sunk into one of the leather armchairs, spreading her skirts carefully. "What I have to say makes no difference, evidently," she said. Her voice was flat, and contained no emotion.

Nigel spoke. "Sara will stay on at Withenshaws. She is not returning to you. You have treated her abominably; this time, she will not forgive you. Even when she has her own child in her arms again, which I hope will be soon, it will be reared with us at Withenshaws. You may do as you will with the gipsy's child which you substituted. I understand that he may be your own. That will at least lend colour to the story that he is your heir, and if Buckler takes a trip out here he may note the resemblance. No, I am not reporting your felony, Francis; let it be on your own conscience."

"My dear Nigel, you are crazed. Have some wine."

"I am neither crazed nor will I drink your wine again. Also, I am taking Belinda back with us. She needs strict keeping, and I will provide it."

"I am not consulted," said Helena languidly. "I would greatly enjoy a little wine with you, Francis; the journey was made in breathless haste, and by the time someone has found and dressed Belinda it will be an hour before we can leave." Her voice rose and fell on the plaintive, harsh note she used when things did not please her. She sipped the wine Francis had poured. He turned away to fill his own glass. His cheeks were flushed slightly.

"What do you expect me to say?" he said. "Sara suffered no such ill-treatment as should have caused her to leave childbed and walk God knows how many miles to Withenshaws."

"She did not have to walk all the way; fortunately, I found her and carried her back."

"You should have brought her back here. What do you

suppose the county will say when it is known that she is living with you, even under Helena's protection?"

"We must hope that they never guess the truth, or notice—as I hope—that there is a little child at Withenshaws and another at Ae."

"And if they do, what will you say to them?"

"Nothing; I shall leave them to draw their own conclusions."

"It has not occurred to you that this whole tale is a farrago of lies, or rather of Sara's fevered imagination?"

"If you say that again I will knock you over."

"You are behaving like a schoolboy, Nigel," said Helena.

He ignored her. "If Belinda is ready—or even if she is not—we had best go, and take her as she is."

Belinda was found, and brought; Helena exclaimed with horror. "She has swelled out like a frog. Do you drive home with her, Nigel; I cannot sit in the same carriage."

"I will escort you, Helena," said Francis.

Nigel had kissed his daughter. Belinda smiled, put her tongue out, and shrank against his side. She hardly knew her mother, seeing her occasionally only as a personage who neither looked at nor spoke to her. Her short-thumbed hand sought Nigel's and he held it.

"We will go, then," he said curtly. He turned and left the room with the child. Presently they heard him driving away.

"A little more wine, Helena, before we go," said Francis. "Then you may like to come up and see the baby. I want you to tell everyone how like me he is. You at least are my friend." He took her hand and kissed it.

"Dear Francis, of course I will come," she said, and when the wine had been drunk he showed her upstairs to the nursery, where the baby, much grown, slept quietly, his brown curls fluffier than they had been at the birth. "Why, he is the very image of you, Francis," said Helena, in clear tones so that the nurse might hear. Afterwards, when they were out again at the head of the stairs, preparing to descend, she leaned towards him.

"What a naughty boy you are!" she whispered in his ear.

Sara had asked that Biddy be brought over to Withenshaws. "She knows my ways and I know hers. Your servants are very well trained, Nigel, much more so than I am."

So Biddy had been sent for and brought back on horseback by one of the footmen, and Sara had the great pleasure of seeing the Irish girl bring in her supper-tray. She ate with more relish now; somehow, everything would come right, and she drained the last of the soup-cup in which the cook's best broth had been ladled. Then Biddy settled her pillows in order that she might sleep; but Sara lay wide-eyed, with a feeling that the day was not done.

She was right. About eleven o'clock there came a discreet tapping at her door. Biddy, who slept in the dressing-room, heard it and flew to answer it; who could want her mistress at this hour? It was one of the correct Withenshaws maids, to say there was a young woman downstairs with a baby, who insisted on seeing Mrs Atherstone tonight.

Biddy went over to the bed and gave the message. "She's not very clean, the maid says," she was trying to add, but already Sara had flown from her bed and towards the door, in bare feet; horrified, Biddy ran after her and cast a dressing-gown about her. But Sara was already at the head of the stairs, holding out her arms to the bedraggled young woman in the hall and the bundle she carried.

"Mary! Mary! Bring her to me, bring her to me!" And she tried to make her way downstairs, but Mary Runcatch had moved swiftly, and was with her before she could clasp the banisters. She put the baby in Sara's arms; the poor little creature was filthy, and smelt of dirt and woodsmoke.

"Meribah," said Sara. She looked down into her daughter's face. The eyes were still shut and the mouth dribbled milk. Sara raised a radiant face. "Biddy, tell them to bring me warm water and a footbath, and a clean shawl if they have one, till her other things are washed," she said. "And, Mary, you must have a hot bath too. Wash your hair and comb it, and tomorrow I'll give you a gown. Tonight will you sleep with Biddy? Will either of you mind? Oh, there is so much to say!"

"Then let's say it, madam," said Mary Runcatch. "*He'll* be after me, sure as fate; he'll know where I've gone, whether here or Ae: I went to Ae first. And he'll never give up searching. I was only able to get away because he'd gone off with some of them and the ponies. No, he never loved me or wanted me, but I was his woman, as he used to say, and he was always at me, never a night's peace." She talked on, as if exhaustion made her careless of the words she used; Sara had a glimpse of a life she had never encountered. She raised her head from bathing the baby's little limbs and said "Bring Miss Bartlett a cup of that good broth, and some bread, and heat water for her. You will feel better tomorrow. And in my gown you will be as you were again. It's brown, and quite plain. It has hardly been worn, and you will feel like you used to, and you will stay here and look after Belinda."

"Oh, madam, madam, I'd like it of all things, but Runcatch—"

"The footmen will deal with him—if he comes. You walked all the way both to Ae and here? You must be exhausted." Sara spared a glance from Meribah to look at the haggard wreck that had once been the seemly governess; her hair straggled and the bones showed through her skin; one eye was discoloured. Sara resolved fiercely at that moment to guard two people; Meribah, and Mary Bartlett. She should be Mary Bartlett again; that marriage had been a travesty.

Meribah was comfortable, clean, and dried, her dark hair beginning to shine. It was quite straight, and her eyes were not yet open. She gave a great yawn as Sara wrapped her in the new shawl. How much better this was than a clay baby!

Next day, Belinda was sent for to see the new arrival. She crooned and laughed, pleased also to see Miss Bartlett back; no one had taken much notice of her since the governess left. She could not stop watching the baby, how it slept and wakened, cried for food, took food, curled and uncurled its tiny fingers. Belinda put out a finger of her own and Meribah grasped it. Belinda laughed and put out her tongue, a real sign of pleasure.

"Baby again," she said on being sent away. "See baby again."

"Yes, darling, see baby again. But she must sleep now."

It was only after she had gone out that Mary turned white-faced to Sara.

"Forgive me—I may be wrong—but I think—I think she is going to have a child."

"*Belinda*? But who would do such a cruel, unnatural thing?"

"Runcatch."

Sara had dismissed everyone, sent for Nigel to come to her alone, put both her arms about his neck, holding him close, and told him.

He lay for moments like her child, against her breast. Then he said "We must obtain confirmation from the doctor. It may not be true. It may be a tumour or—simply the thickening due to her age. We must pray that that is all. But Helena is the girl's mother and I must tell her."

"Yes," she agreed. "You must tell Helena. Would it be easier if I were there—if you told her up here—where she can see the baby? Perhaps—" She did not really know what she meant to say next; that the sight of a normal, beautiful baby might soften Helena, make her less bitter. On the other hand, it might make everything worse.

Helena came when she was sent for. She kept up a valiant pretence that all was as it should be, that Sara's visit was only temporary. The baby she did not try to explain; in fact she hardly looked at it. Gently, Nigel told her about Belinda.

"Ugh," said Helena. "Ugh. What kind of monster would she produce? I have always said she should be shut away, and now you see I was right. Running free about Ae, any farmhand could lay her on her back. I cannot understand how anyone would want to touch her, even a man. You must send her away to an institution. If she stays here, *I* will leave." The blue eyes sent a malicious glance to Sara, lying in the bed with her baby by her. "The county will talk then," she said, "wont' they, Nigel?"

"You may stay or go as you choose. Belinda stays here, at her home, where we love her and will care for her."

"And care for the newt, or whatever it is she produces? You have a bigger heart than mine, Nigel."

"I have always known that."

She turned about, sweeping her skirts with her; and went from the room. When they were alone Nigel went back to

Sara, taking her in his arms and comforting her; she was shivering and crying like a child.

"Hush," he said, "hush. You will do the baby harm. Think of the baby always. Think of Meribah."

"I wish that she were yours," she said.

"Perhaps some day you may bear me a child. Would you do so?"

"Yes, with all my heart."

It was then that they heard the servant screaming, from the hall at the foot of the stairs. "The mistress! The mistress! She's tripped and fallen down, all the way. Her neck's broke. It looks like she's dead."

Nigel pressed Sara to him, then hurried away. Seen from the top of the staircase Helena's body was a grotesque huddle, with the head at a twisted angle; the shining head that had so well matched the curtains.

Belinda was hiding in a cupboard, because she knew that what she had done was wrong. She had been waiting outside the door to see the baby again—she loved, always and always, to see the baby—and she had heard what they said. Monster. Newt. Shut away. Institution. She did not know what the words meant, but she knew her mother meant her harm. It had been simple to kill her, although Belinda's thoughts had not ranged so far. When the tall figure with the shining hair swept past her on the balcony, and began to descend the stair, Belinda ran out and gave her a strong push. There was in fact great strength in those pink, plump arms with their strange hands. Helena had not been grasping the rail, and losing her balance she fell, down and down, her skirts whirling, like—if Belinda had known—the fallen angels, like leaves in Vallombrosa.

Then she had lain very still. And Belinda had retired to her cupboard.

They sent for the doctor. Nigel had meanwhile ordered that no one was to disturb the body and had flung a sheet over it. Until the doctor arrived he stood guard over what had been his wife. He was aware of no feeling except shock; one moment Helena had been alive, malevolent, and now she was stilled for ever. He must ensure in the future that no one else tripped on the staircase.

Lanterns and the scrape of carriage wheels announced the doctor's arrival. He came in, non-committal as usual. "I am sorry to hear of this, Consett," he said. He knelt down, removed the sheet, and examined the dead woman's neck. "A clean fracture, upper cervical. There is also a contusion on the head where a balustrade post may have struck it. Otherwise she would feel no pain."

"I am glad of that." What else was one to say? Even to Helena, one would not have wished suffering.

"Did you see it happen? Did anyone?" The doctor's blue eyes had narrowed. One must never rule out the possibility of foul play; and it had been rumoured for long that Consett and his wife were not on the best of terms.

"I cannot answer for the servants. I myself saw nothing. I was in the upper bedroom at the time, talking to a visitor, when we heard the maid screaming."

"How long had your wife's body lain there?"

"Perhaps five or six minutes. She had left us recently to go downstairs."

"And you did not accompany her?"

"I have already said that I was engaged in talk with a visitor."

"Could your visitor have seen anything?"

"Impossible. She was in bed, and had been there all day."

"May I see her?"

"By all means. It is Mrs Atherstone. She has been here for two days."

"*Mrs Atherstone*? But she is in childbed at Ae."

"Certain considerations induced her to leave Ae."

"She should not have travelled in her state. May I see her briefly?"

"By all means."

Nigel waited by Helena's body until the doctor came out of Sara's room. He descended the stairs thoughtfully and said "Last time I saw Mrs Atherstone she was in great distress, at Ae, refusing to feed her son. Now I find her contentedly feeding her daughter. The situation is, you will admit, a little odd. I had heard her story, which might have been delirium."

"But has no connection with my wife's death."

"No, but some explanation—"

"An explanation can be made easily. Mrs Atherstone's husband replaced the daughter to whom she had just given birth with the son of the coachman's wife, of whom we suspect he is the father. She—Mrs Atherstone—was in great distress."

"I saw her. She told me."

"Next day she rose and dressed herself and started to walk here to Withenshaws. I happened to be out riding and brought her here. Later, the coachman's wife came back here also, to give back the girl baby which belonged to Mrs Atherstone."

"And where, in all this, is Mr Atherstone?"

"He will have to be informed of my wife's death. They were very close."

"Did you, Mr Consett, dislike or resent your wife enough to have pushed her down those stairs? I ask because the police may have to ask. I am not sure that I can issue a certificate."

"You must do as you think fit. We had not lived as man and wife for many years, but tolerated one another. There would have been no reason for me suddenly to murder Helena, as you imply."

"Not even with Mrs Atherstone and her child under your roof?"

"Not even so."

"Yet your wife left the room, it seems, hurriedly—or at least not slowly enough to guard herself while descending the stairs."

"There was something which had upset and annoyed her; a matter on which I had intended consulting you shortly. We believe my daughter, Belinda, to be pregnant. As you know, she is a mongol. The news upset my wife, as I say."

"Had she great affection for Belinda?"

"She had none."

The doctor turned and looked once more at what had been Helena Consett. Then he said quietly "When, with your assent, I talked for a few moments with Mrs Atherstone, I did not upset her."

"I accept your assurance."

The doctor had left. Nigel gave orders for all the servants to stay in their quarters; the body could not be moved until the police had been. Sara wondered about Francis. "He will want to be informed; he *must* be informed." The thought of Francis' riding over here, making violent scenes and accusations, made her quail; but he had loved Helena.

"He shall be, and by me; but I think we should wait for the police investigation. He can see her then as she used to be, properly coffined, and can remember her so. I fear the sight of her now would drive him mad."

He was sitting by her bed, and they held hands. "Stay with me," she said. The baby was sound asleep; they had found a cradle for it in one of the attics.

"I will stay. I could not sleep, alone in the dark; and neither could you. What *did* happen?"

They were not left long in doubt. Mary had gone off in search of Belinda; it was as though she had assumed her old mantle of governess easily. Presently the sound of a carriage indicated the arrival of the police. Nigel rose and went down. There were two of them, who introduced themselves formally; a detective-inspector and a detective-sergeant. They went straight to the body, knelt down to examine it, and then took measurements; afterwards there would be a gruesome chalk line where Helena had lain on the floor. Presently they nodded. "You may have her taken into a side room now, if you wish," they said. "It is no doubt inconvenient not to use the hall."

Nigel nodded, and led the way to a small sitting-room where there was a sofa on which Helena had often lain. They laid her there now, the twisted neck causing her face to be turned away into the cushions. Nigel replaced the sheet, and lit a lamp.

"We'll not need that, sir," said one of the police officers. Nigel looked at him. "She will be alone in the dark long enough," he said. "While she may, she shall have light."

"You were fond of your wife, sir? Forgive me, it's a routine question."

"No. Our relations had not been good for many years—in fact, since our only child was born. She is mentally defective and my wife blamed me. Since then, although we shared a house, we have led separate lives."

"Well, that's honest, sir. Where is the little girl now?"

"Her governess is looking for her; she ran off somewhere. This house is strange to her: she is used to live at Ae, with my cousin."

"Who else lives here?"

"Myself and the servants; and recently, my cousin's wife and her baby."

The police looked at one another. "She is staying as a friend of your wife, no doubt?"

"No; my wife and she were not on good terms. You will see that I am telling you the whole truth, inspector; I am as bewildered as anyone. Mrs Atherstone is here as a friend of my own; in fact, she came to me for shelter."

"And brought your daughter and the governess?"

"No, they arrived separately."

"Was there some happening at Ae that caused four persons suddenly to leave it?"

Nigel frowned. "Forgive me, but does that have any bearing on my wife's death?"

"It may have, if your wife's death was not accidental."

"I can assure you that one person, in that case, who is innocent is Mrs Atherstone. She had been put to bed, with her baby by her, and was talking to me when we heard the servant scream out that my wife was dead."

"But there was time, before the servant came, for someone to ensure that your wife *was* dead, Mr Consett."

"That is true. All I know are my own movements, and those of Mrs Atherstone. She will verify what I say, but of course we could have arranged that. All I ask is that, if you interview her, you do not upset her; she has only recently given birth to her child."

"What was your wife's reaction to Mrs Atherstone's coming here?"

"She came upstairs, saw the baby, and then I broke some news to her which was unwelcome to her. She took it very badly, and swept out of the room. That was the last time we saw her alive."

"Did the news concern yourself and Mrs Atherstone?" It was evident that the inspector was following a specific trail.

"No, it concerned my daughter, and does not concern this case."

"I think that it does, if it incurred your wife's displeasure and caused her to hurry from the room. She may no doubt have taken the stairs hastily, tripped perhaps—who knows?—and fallen; at any rate she was not in a calm state when she went down."

"That is true. My wife was generally a calm person, not given to showing her feelings."

"I put it to you again that her upset concerned Mrs Atherstone."

"And I continue to deny it."

"Do you refuse to tell me the nature of the news that upset your wife?"

"For others' sake, yes—unless it becomes vitally necessary, which I do not think it will."

The men exchanged glances again. "Perhaps we may interview Mrs Atherstone now."

"May I be present?"

"We should prefer to interview her alone. We will do our utmost not to upset her, as you ask."

"Then I will show you her room."

He had mounted the stairs in front of them; and was about to turn the handle of Sara's door when a dishevelled Belinda, led by Mary, broke away and ran to him, hiding her face in his coat. Nigel bent down to her, speaking to her tenderly.

"Why, where has my girl been?"

"I found her in a cupboard," said Mary. "She was covered with cobwebs and dust." She made a small acknowledgment to the police officers. "I think that she has something to say which will put an end to your investigation. Belinda, tell Papa what you have just told me."

Belinda burrowed more deeply into her father's arms. "Tell them," he said gently. He had already guessed the nature of the confession.

"Not tell. B'linda bad."

"If Belinda was bad, it may hurt aunty. Tell these gentlemen what happened. Belinda say. No one angry."

She raised a tear-stained, dust-streaked face. "B'linda bad. Pushed mama downstairs." The tight-lidded eyes stared at the two strange men. The inspector, a family man, knelt down by her.

"Why, Belinda," he said, "did you do that?"

She backed away. "Not like mama."

Nigel intervened. "May I speak, sir? I think that Belinda may have heard some of the things my wife was saying to me and to Mrs Atherstone, of whom she is fond. My wife was suggesting, as she has done before, that Belinda should be put in an institution. Belinda has heard that often enough, perhaps, to know what it means. Was that why, Belinda?"

Belinda nodded vigorously. The police retreated almost visibly from the centre of the stage. How could one bring this poor child into court? The inspector turned to Nigel.

"I think, sir, that unless fresh evidence comes to light we may abandon the case. But I suggest that you have your daughter closely guarded and do not leave her alone."

"Miss Bartlett will see to that," said Nigel thankfully. "I am glad—very glad—that the truth has come out. For myself I thought Helena had caught her foot and tripped, though it was unlikely in that case that she would have fallen all the way."

"That was what was troubling us, sir," said the inspector.

When they had gone Nigel went at once to Sara. "It's all over, my darling—all over—" He knelt by the side of her bed and covered his face in his hands. "I should feel grief, shame, God knows what," he said. "But I only feel relief that she is gone and that the news about Belinda need not become public property. No more will be heard of it, I am certain."

A knock came at the door; it was Mary. "May Belinda come in to say goodnight?" she asked. "She is—disturbed. It would calm her if you kissed her."

Belinda, washed and in her nightgown, came hesitantly in. "B'linda bad," she said. Her mouth drooped and there was no sign of her tongue.

"Look at the baby," Sara told her. "See her cradle! You can rock it with your foot. Mary, show her."

Mary rocked gently, and Belinda rocked wildly; presently they had to stop her or the baby would have been flung awake. They took her on to Sara's bed and made a fuss of her for a little while. Aside, Nigel spoke to the governess.

"When you take her downstairs for a day or two, don't go by the hall. I don't know yet whether or not we are permitted to remove that damned chalk line. The sooner her mind is filled with other things the better. Can you do it, do you think? Mr Francis will be coming tomorrow, and there may be unpleasantness. Her mother's body is in the little sitting-room, and there will be the undertakers and then the funeral. Keep her away from all that, at the back of the house."

"I will try," said Mary.

After she had gone Sara looked down at Nigel's head, once more laid against her. She said gently "And now, my love, you must write to poor Francis. Write now, and send it in the morning; that way you will sleep."

The undertakers were busy when Francis rode over next day. He was wild-eyed and his clothes were flung on carelessly; his breath smelt of brandy. He alighted from his horse, strode up to Nigel and took him by the lapels of his coat. "You killed her," he said. "You killed her."

"Not so, Francis. Come inside, and you shall see her. I did not kill her, I swear it. Why should I do so after all these years?"

"Because of Sara. Because of my wife. She's here, isn't she? The two of you were in it together, got Helena and threw her downstairs to her death." He began to sob tearlessly, like a man in shock, as he was. "Come with me," said Nigel. "You shall see Sara; but you must be gentle with her, for the baby is newly born. How could she have flung anyone downstairs?"

"Yet she got to you. She got to you."

"I found her on the way, and carried her here." He was guiding Francis up the steps; the latter still sobbed, and struck Nigel's arm away petulantly.

"I will see her. I will see Helena now. Oh my love, Helena! You never loved her. You took her from me and you never loved her. She should have married me. If it hadn't been for the money—"

"All that is old, old history," said Nigel gently. He had coaxed Francis into the hall. The other's eyes started from their sockets and he screamed. "What is that? What in the world is that? Is that how they found her?"

"It is a chalk line. The police made it. She is not like that now."

"The police? The police were here? Then it *was* murder."

"They have been here, and have left again, bringing no case. Your mind may be easy. Presently you shall see Helena again, beautiful as you have ever seen her. Come now and visit Sara and your child. Do not withdraw from us any more, Francis. We feel as you do. We would help you if you would let us. Come."

He felt a shade of unease as he led Francis into Sara's room; but at least he was there to protect her and the baby. To his surprise, Sara held up her face to Francis. "I know how sad you feel," she said. "We are your friends, Francis; do you be ours."

He had kissed her, as of routine duty; but it was an advance. Sara pointed to the baby's cot. "That is our baby," she said. "Mary brought her back to me. Francis, would you like me to rear yours with her? That way, he would not be an only child, perhaps lonely, at Ae. What have you called him?"

"Nicholas."

"And has Nicholas the proper nurses and folk to feed and bathe and dress him? It can all be done here, when we see to Meribah."

"Meribah . . . the waters of bitterness. I did not mean, when I said that to you, that you should use the name. It is ugly."

"It is ugly and yet I felt it was the right name. She is like you, do you not think?"

"Sara . . . I have treated you badly . . ."

"Not that, so much as that you did not love me. You loved Helena, and she knew of it. One cannot help these things. Presently you shall see her. Let us all be friends together; that I beg."

"You and Nigel . . ."

"Yes, I and Nigel; the same as you and Helena. A great many things go wrong in this world; we cannot always have our own way when we are young. But now we are not so young, and wiser. Bring Nicholas to Withenshaws, and ride over and see him whenever you like; why not?"

A knock had come to the door; it was the undertaker. Nigel went to answer it and returned.

"We may see her now," he said. "Francis shall go first."

He guided Francis down to the place where the open coffin lay, and left him alone.

Francis returned in a little while; he had been weeping. "She is so pale," he said, "so pale. And her hair shines like gold. I never saw a more beautiful woman; and she had to die."

Sara looked at Nigel, who shook his head. He would not go down to view the dead. They would have turned out the lamp; daylight had come. Someone had removed the chalk marks in the hall.

The funeral was well attended; Helena had had many social contacts. Sara came—she was strong enough now—and sat in the church between Nigel and Francis. A part of her mind wryly recognised that, here between them, she would silence any gossip that might have arisen. When the service was over she let the two men go out to act as pall-bearers, and sat on, with her head bowed. Afterwards, at the lych-gate, several women spoke to her. She answered briefly, correctly; the days of the *farouche* potter-woman were done. She must live for the children now, for Francis and for Nigel.

Sara was wearing the mourning-clothes that had been bought for Helena's funeral, and Biddy had already brought her underclothes and night-things from Ae. Nevertheless there were still some items to be fetched, and Sara thought she would not accompany the party in the carriage. Belinda, as a treat, went with her father, and Biddy again joined them to pack and bring back the remaining gear. Sara stayed in the drawing-room at Withenshaws, and Mary stayed in the house also, but kept to her upstairs room. "It will be a holiday for you to be free of Belinda for a little while," Sara said. She herself was not fully restored to strength after the baby's birth, tired easily, and was glad of rest and quiet in this room, furnished by Helena; and yet Helena's presence seemed no longer to cling to it, or to anything at Withenshaws. Perhaps if her spirit were unquiet she would haunt Ae.

"What nonsense I am thinking," Sara told herself, and closed her eyes and prepared to doze, a little, till the others returned. She was glad that the enmity of Francis seemed to be at an end. He would no doubt talk with Nigel of old days, pour him wine, detain him long after Biddy was ready to come back. As for Belinda, she would know where she was again; would roam through the yard and stables, perhaps climb to the apple-loft. Sara shuddered; in one of those places Runcatch had been used to await her. She was suddenly aware of imminent danger, merely at the thought of his name; and thrust down the notion as though it had been folly. It *was* folly; she was in no way psychic, and neither Helena's ghost nor Runcatch's memory should affect her. Yet the feeling remained.

After a little while she decided that she would go for a short walk; not too far, merely to exercise her muscles after lying in bed. She took a stout stick from among those in the hall, and set out in her black dress, hatless.

It was not cold; she walked round the garden in front, and then along the grass-grown paths that led to the stables and outbuildings at the back. It came to her that she had never been into these; Withenshaws had once had its own dairy, and there was a steading where they had kept and milked the cows. She explored the dairy, thinking of her studio at Ae and wondering if she would ever have the leisure to make pottery sometimes at Withenshaws. If so, this place would be ideal, as in the way of old dairies there was a little stream running through the middle of the channelled floor, for scouring and cleansing utensils.

The light flooded through the opposite door, which was open, and in an instant she saw it darkened. She stayed rigid, aware that to scream aloud would be both foolish and dangerous. Runcatch stood there, in the tattered leather coat horse-dealers wear.

She confronted him and he her; their eyes met and challenged one another. Then he turned, and went, without a word spoken. Sara felt her knees trembling with shock; she did not remember getting herself back to the house, to her room.

"I did not tell her. It would only have frightened her without cause; she would have felt it dangerous to leave the house, to go anywhere alone."

"But it *is* dangerous, unless he means her no harm. I think she should at least be warned that he is near the house, looking for her."

Nigel was frowning, so that his handsome face was spoiled. "Well, I will tell her," said Sara. "However he may just have meant to have a word about something—but in that case why did he not speak? It was his silence that was so terrible."

"I will warn every manservant in the place that if he is seen here, he is to be taken immediately. And I think our friends the police should be informed. He may be wanted for other things than ill-treating his wife and purloining your baby."

"To think that he drove the coach at Ae all that time, and looked like nothing more than a respectable coachman! We could all have had our throats cut."

"Or your purses. Francis must be warned. It is possible that the man may approach him for more money."

"I will go and warn Mary, as you ask it," Sara said, and Nigel looked down at her tenderly.

"You need not climb the stairs; you are tired enough. I will send one of the servants to bring her."

When Mary came he had already gone out of the room, leaving the two women to confront one another. Mary's appearance had altered completely; with the interval of food, rest and self-respect, she was again the unremarkable governess who shadowed Belinda. But when she heard the news she turned pale.

"If he's after me, nothing will stop him. He means to kill me, that I know."

"Why should he kill you, Mary? No doubt he only wants you to go back to him. I should perhaps have said this afternoon that you will not go."

Mary had not moved; she was standing with her hands by her sides, like a woman who had heard nothing. "It doesn't matter, madam," she said. "If Runcatch is out to get me, he will. There is no use in hiding from it or making what's left of life miserable because of it. You've made me happy here, and I'll go on that way as long as it's left to me."

"At least promise not to go out of the house without a servant to attend you, and a heavy stick to protect yourself."

"Very well. I'll promise that." But she spoke tonelessly, as if it meant nothing.

Christmas was drawing near, and Francis had been invited to Christmas dinner. Sara, who was gradually learning cookery lore, had gone to see the cook about the stuffing; before that, she, Mary and Belinda had been cutting out coloured paper decorations for the Christmas tree. Nicholas, the Ae baby, slumbered upstairs with Meribah. Outside it was cold, but without snow.

They had had great fun with the patterns, amazing themselves at what they could achieve with a fold there, a snip there; stars and wheels and bells hung ready pinned upon the tall spruce, which one of the Ae servants had brought over as a present from Francis. There were to be presents for everyone, and a bran tub; this was not to be brought in till the last moment, as Belinda delighted in dipping her hands in it and scattering it over the carpet.

She was very big; no one could tell when the birth would take place. It had been decided among all of them not to fuss or worry the child, to help her when the time came, and to see what she gave birth to then before taking decisions; it might be a normal baby, it might not. In any case it would take its place upstairs meantime in the nursery among the other babies. Sara once looked back at her own impatient days at the dame-school, and wondered at herself now; there was nothing she would not have done for any of the children.

Mary snipped silently, producing the cleverest shapes. She had shown no particular interest in Nicholas when he arrived, curly-haired and sturdy. It was as though she had shed that brief span of her life like a snake its skin, and would neither balk at meeting Francis nor at anything else, even the worst of all. Since she knew Runcatch had come looking for her she had acquired a strange calm, like that of a saint in a church window. She and Sara had not spoken of it again after the first telling.

Suddenly Belinda gave a cry, dropped the scissors and paper and began rubbing her stomach. Mary came over to her, felt her, and felt the unborn child move. Belinda was crying now, as one will who does not understand pain. She had never endured it before, thought Mary. She stayed with Belinda and tried to hold her in her arms; but Belinda wrenched away, still crying, and ran out of the room, Mary after her. She ran out of the door into the cold world outside, without hat or coat; the child's stout stockinged legs were well ahead of her; she could hear the sobbing and wailing, and knew that Belinda thought she was running away from it, towards the things she knew and understood.

"Belinda! Belinda!" But Belinda had taken the road to Ae, as though returning to the womb. On the way the waters burst, and Mary came upon them as she hurried after, and the trail they left; the birth would not be long. "Belinda! Belinda darling! Wait for me!" But nothing would make Belinda wait; a fear she had never known was with her, and pain, pain; it came in spasms, so that sometimes she would think it gone, then it would start again, and the whole of her body was wrenched with it, and she did not know why.

There was a force, one she did not understand, moving, thrusting within her; she pushed against her stomach to try and stop it, then ran on; in her limited mind was a picture of Ae, which she knew and where she had understood everything; once she was at Ae she would be safe. The road wound greyly, and she struggled on; then the pain became so fierce she could only lie in the road and groan, her face turned to the hedge.

"Belinda. Belinda." Mary had caught up with her at last, her voice breathless. "Do not be frightened, darling. Let me hold you. Soon you will have a little baby, like Nicholas, like Meribah." As she spoke she prayed that she was right; what monster might now be produced? The wailing and sobbing went on; Belinda was in great pain, here on the cold road with none but herself to aid her. Mary began to shiver, lacking her coat; she could not carry Belinda back to Withenshaws, she was too heavy.

The sound of horse's hooves came; Mary stood up in the road and signalled wildly. At that moment she had forgotten her own constant fear; whoever came must help. It was the doctor, busy on his rounds. He stopped and alighted. Mary blurted out her tale, and he knelt down by the child in labour. Then he looked up, his eyes blue as ever against the grey day.

"I cannot take two of you on my horse, but I will carry her back to Withenshaws and see her put to bed, and stay with her, while you follow on foot. Who could have done such a thing to her? Whoever they are, they deserve to hang."

This time, Mary did not mention Runcatch.

Sara stayed by Belinda in bed; the doctor had left, saying he would return in two hours. No one could say for how long it would go on; Belinda howled like a tormented animal, a rain of tears running down her scarlet cheeks. For some time, Sara forgot about Mary, then it seemed as if she ought to have come back by now; perhaps she had. Sara went to the door to enquire of one of the servants. No, nobody had come.

Sara began to feel disquiet. Nigel was away in Brede, or he would have ridden out; as it was, she hesitated to give orders quite yet to the men to go and search. There might be quite a simple explanation; perhaps Mary had even met someone on the way and stopped for a moment's talk.

That had happened. An arm had seized hers as she half walked, half ran along the road, her breath coming quickly. The arm was strong and pulled her across the road, into the wood. The other hand closed over her mouth.

Nigel came home. By that time Sara had sent to men-servants out to look. It was early dark and not easy to see without lanterns. Nigel went out again himself with another party of men, armed with sticks and Nigel's pistol. They hunted till past midnight, but there was still no snow to trace prints, although it had grown bitterly cold.

Next day, Nigel informed the police. They brought out a posse of men. They found Mary's body in the wood, frozen as stiff as the beech leaves which persisted from last year. She had been raped and strangled.

Meantime, at midnight, Belinda's child had at last been born. It was a girl, and killed the mother.

"Love? I—I cannot think of it now, after *that*. It will be the same all my life, I think. That animal—and the act the same—it is the same with everyone of us—what else have *we* lain and done, in bed, all winter?"

"And will lie and do again, for your talk is foolish. Because one man makes ugliness out of beauty it does not mean that beauty is destroyed. I will come to you tonight, and show you otherwise."

"No—no—not yet—"

"Then if I may not come tonight, I will take you now. Sara, you must not let dread and horror drive you mad. What happened was ugly and cruel; we all know it. But now, I still love you and I believe you love me. Do you no longer love me because of what happened to Mary and Belinda?"

"I love you—as much as I can anyone—but something has happened to my mind—"

"And I will cure it by loving your body. Come."

He picked her up, carried her to the rug by the fire, went back to the door and locked it. Then he returned to her. At first he only kissed her; her shut eyes, her throat, her mouth and hair, the place behind her ear where the skin was softest. She felt him open her bodice and draw up her skirts. She tried to resist, but he lay upon her.

"Nigel—Nigel—no—"

"Quietly," he said, "I will be gentle," and entered her. So slowly did he move in her that they might have been underwater creatures, soothed by the tides. When her climax came at last she cried out loudly, and felt his lips on hers again, silencing her.

"Hush, love, you'll bring the servants." She heard him, and laughed; it seemed now as if all of her were made of laughter, her body a rush of joy and delight; sometimes before she had felt it so with him, but never so strongly as today. He held firm, and let her ecstasy go by; then he kissed her and said "Now kiss me. Do it with your lips open. I can feel your tears on my face; kiss them away."

And she kissed him; kissed him for the love that she after all bore him, for in the two who had died there had been none of such love; in her times with Francis there had been none. Men and women lived who would never know love, would be born and copulate and marry and bear and die, not knowing it. Yet she, Sara, knew the magic now.

She said in a small voice "Nigel, why do you love me?"

"Why not?" He was laughing, his eyes full of dancing lights. She said, putting up a hand and stroking his face, "I'm not beautiful, or witty or talented except for the clay. Yet you love me; I know you do. You weren't pretending then."

"I was married for many years to the most beautiful woman in the world, and it meant nothing to me. You? I love your green eyes; I love your spirit, your courage, your response. Will that do? Let me kiss you again, and then let us make love again, and make love, and make love . . ."

The little girl who had been born to Belinda was tiny, but perfect. She appeared normal, but the doctor advised waiting for up to a year to see how soon she learned to walk, to speak, to take her own food. In appearance she was a fairy; after the first day, when her hair dried, it was like pale gold shells all over her head; when her eyes opened they remained blue. It seemed that she would look like Helena. Neither of them mentioned it to Francis, whom they had not seen since that unhappy Christmas and who was spending much of his time in London. Ae was neglected; sometimes Sara would drive over and look at the bulbs she had set last year in her garden; they were spreading, daffodils and crocuses, snowdrops, the early growing things. Soon it would be time to weed and plant, but she did not like to assume that Francis would be pleased to think of her at Ae, whether or not he were absent.

As for the pottery, she never looked near it; she might not have known how to handle clay.

Sara's evidence, given to the police, of the date and time she had seen Runcatch in the grounds of Withenshaws was useful, because when they found him at a horse-fair in the north, after some months' search, he denied having been in the south for over a year. After intensive questioning he began to bluster and then broke down. They brought him to London and hanged him.

By that time, Sara, Nigel, Francis and the children were at Ae. Francis had returned in early summer, with lines of dissipation round his eyes and mouth. He could no longer bear Ae alone, he said; would they all come back to live with him?

Sara's green eyes gave him a direct look. "You do not mind that Nigel and I are lovers?" she asked him. Nigel sat silent, watching her; if she did not want to go back to Ae, she should not. Yet the sadness there had been at Withenshaws had destroyed its charm for him; he would be glad enough to go, if Sara—

Francis smiled, and spread out his hands. "I loved Nigel's wife," he said. "Perhaps it is only fair that Nigel should love mine. And the polite world will be nonplussed if we are all under the same roof. I defy any dowager to espy a chink in our armour."

"Sara will be able to do her pottery again," said Nigel.

"With three in the nursery, and—" She blushed. "I had not told Nigel yet. I am to have his child, perhaps in October."

Nigel rose and kissed her. "We have quite a miscellany," said Francis, "like Lady Oxford."

"I am glad that the child will be born at Ae," said Sara. "I loved the house from the first moment I saw it. Oh, I have been happy at Withenshaws, in spite of everything that's happened; but Ae . . . Ae has my heart." She smiled, and looked at Nigel. "Do you not think, my love, that we should drink a toast to Ae?"

And they did so, in the best Mouton de Rothschild from the cellar. Before he left, Sara took Francis by the hand and led him up to the nursery to see Belinda's daughter. He knelt down by the cradle and gazed at the child. "She is Helena over again," he said. "Did you call her that?"

"No, we called her Dorothy."

"I feel like royalty in the Middle Ages," said Sara, watching Nigel handle the reins of the carriage. "They were forever moving from palace to palace to clean out the one they'd left."

"I hope the same reason doesn't apply to Withenshaws," he said, "or the Overtons will complain." He had let Withenshaws for a year; that would be time enough to discover whether or not, now, after all that had happened, Francis and the rest of them could comfortably live together under one roof. If so, he would sell the other house in due course. Now, however, he had ceased to worry about the problem; the day was fine, the scent of pine-needles was blown towards them on the breeze as they approached Ae, and may-blossom was white in the hedgerows.

Suddenly there was a shot. It came from not far off, in the hedge field. Nigel clapped his hand to his head. "I'm all right," he said to Sara, who had clutched his arm in terror. "I want to stop and see who fired that. they may have been after hares; but they should be more careful."

She begged him not to stop. "There is a hole in the crown of your hat," she said. "For God's sake drive on as quickly as you can; we can send one of the Ae servants out to ask who was shooting here today."

"As you please," he said. When they reached Ae and he removed his tall hat, it was to find a peppering of shot-holes in the crown. He called to Francis hastily; might he send a couple of men to look into the field?

"By all means, my dear fellow. What an unpleasant thing to happen. They may, as you say, have been shooting hares; it's the kind of shot a poacher uses. But I think you should inform the police."

"So do I," said Sara, who was trembling. "An inch or two lower and it would have killed you. They weren't shooting hares; the aim was too high."

The two serving-men returned with no information about anyone found in the field or the near district. The police were informed, came to Ae, took notes, and departed saying they would investigate. "That means nothing," said Sara. All her pleasure at returning to Ae had been destroyed by the small incident. She could not forget Runcatch, mouldering now in quicklime in a gaol graveyard; he would have had brothers, perhaps, relatives who would maintain a vendetta as the Corsicans did, the Italians. She said nothing to Nigel or Francis of it, but was in an agony of fear whenever Nigel went out.

Nothing more happened meantime; but Colonel Overton, the tenant of Withenshaws, rode across one day for an informal visit. Over the wine he said, "You have some rough-looking characters in the district, Consett. I came on one the other day, in the grounds. He said he was a horse-dealer, but I asked him what the devil he was doing at Withenshaws. Then he got truculent. 'What's that to do with ya?' he said, and I pointed out that I was after all the tenant and responsible to yourself. I asked him if his name was Runcatch—you remember that case, of course, and the trial was in the papers. 'It may be, and it may not,' he said, 'and in either case it's none of your affair.' I sent him packing, but I feel glad of my dogs; they'd have made short shrift of him if they'd been out, but they were kennelled."

"We'll get ourselves a guard dog," said Francis resolutely. "I myself used to be so often away that it would have been unfair to the brute, but now my wife and my cousin are established here with the children there will always be somebody at Ae."

The Colonel gazed into his wineglass. There had been curious gossip, he knew, about the relations here between husband, wife and cousin. Mrs Atherstone was not present, but he'd seen her in church; a handsome woman enough, not one to remember with any clarity. And the husband—perhaps a *mari complaisant*? If so it was no business of his, and he'd tell his wife not to spread conjecture about it when he got back home. They all lived together without ill-feeling, that was evident; and nobody wanted feuds and quarrels in the district. He took his leave shortly, having been shown the hat with the holes and warned to guard himself. "I think, however, that you are safe," Nigel told him. "If anyone is the selected victim it is myself, for bringing Runcatch to the rope's end. An eye for an eye, perhaps; and it damned nearly was." He smiled, and the visitor departed with the memory of that pleasant smile. Anything he could do for his landlord would be a pleasure. Consett was a good fellow. Atherstone seemed sullen by nature, a trifle, but not enough to do harm. Soon, no doubt, he and his wife would be invited to dine at Ae, and then there could be a closer look at Mrs Atherstone. My word, he was getting like an old woman or a hen! But that business of the shots had been mysterious. If the police knew their duty, they would move the gipsies on.

Colonel Overton's wife was French—he had met her while spending a furlough in Nice—and had brought with her a French maid named Sidonie. Sidonie had the great advantage that while she was deft at every aspect of her required art, and could dress hair like a dream, she herself was unlikely ever to marry. This was because of a singular misfortune; she possessed a beard. It is true that Frenchmen, and Latin lovers of all kinds, accord moderate approval to a *soupçon* of dark down on the upper lip or eyebrows joined by dark hair in the manner of the ancient Greeks. But a beard is not the same thing. Sidonie did her best; shying away from the indignity of having to shave like a man, she used scissors, tweezers, waxes, and every available aid, all to no purpose; the more the beard was attacked the thicker it seemed to grow, and as she was now thirty, she had given up trying to conquer it and had simply developed a habit of wearing her cloak collar high up against her face when out. Her life, which had begun in Nantes, had been free of admirers, and she had grown both sour and cautious.

It so happened that the gingerbread fair, held once every five years near Brede, was to be held this year, and Sidonie's mistress gave her permission to go. She was escorted there in the Overton carriage, which was going further on, and told that she must be at a certain spot in two hours' time for the return lift home. Left to herself, Sidonie looked about her with a distinct sense of disappointment. There was very little to see, apart from the gingerbread stalls and a few dusty ponies grazing on the littered grass: no whirling horses on a roundabout, no fortune-teller, no tumbling clowns. The people who had come seemed rough, none above the servant class; evidently those of high degree did not patronise the fair. Sidonie bought herself a piece of hot gingerbread and munched it, standing a little way back on the grass, looking at the hooded wagons in which the perpetrators of the fair must live. Presently she found that she was being watched also; and in a little while a slim man, with a greyhound by him, sidled up to her. Sidonie's dark eyes prepared a rebuff; she had always been respectable. However the newcomer addressed her so humbly, and appeared to know who she was, that Sidonie had not the heart to turn him away; after all, he was someone to talk to.

"You are the maid of Madame, Madame Overton?" The man might almost have been French himself; but he was not. Sidonie admitted her identity.

"I often watch you in the carriage going to church," he said. "Your mistress dresses very beautifully. Is she a good mistress?"

"I would not have been with her as long as I have if she had not been," replied Sidonie, who in course of her years of duty had picked up English almost free of any accent.

The stranger smiled.

"You have wit, I see. Do you like it here? Do you find it lonely?"

"Why do you ask, *monsieur*? It is nothing to you whether I am lonely or not."

"On the other hand, it means a great deal. I have admired you for a long time. Will you walk round the fair with me, and I will show you some of the sights that ordinary visitors do not see? It is a pity you have bought that gingerbread; my mother makes the best, and I would have got some for you from her for nothing."

The combination of compliment and respectability—after all he had mentioned his mother—overcame Sidonie's scruples and she let him take her arm in his. The greyhound accompanied them. It was also true that he showed her things she might not have found for herself, being too timid to go into all the tents; a lady with nothing but a head; two dwarfs, a rather mangy bear that danced, and a seller of medicines reputed to cure everything. Sidonie thought at once of her beard and brought out her purse to buy a bottle, but the gallant escort was before her, and paid for it, saw it wrapped handsomely, and presented it to her with a bow.

"But, *monsieur*, you are not to give me presents," said Sidonie, whose upbringing had taught her that if one accepted a gift from a man it meant that he would, or should, propose marriage by way of her parents. The man with the greyhound smiled. "Do not be alarmed," he said. "I wanted to do something for you, because I greatly hope you will do something for me. May I tell you what it is?"

Visions of lost virginity flitted across Sidonie's mind, but after all they were in broad daylight and in public. "You may tell me, but I promise nothing," she said, and remembered that he had not told her his name. That was an omission, and she asked for it. He smiled, showing irregular white teeth.

"They call me Dandy Jack, because when I like I can speak like a gentleman," he said. "I have been speaking like one to you. When I am among my own family you would not understand a word I said—well, perhaps one in ten—because I speak as they do. But for you I take trouble."

"What is it you want me to do for you?" She was still suspicious.

"I want you, if you will, to procure me a sheet of the writing-paper your mistress uses, and an envelope; and to copy out this letter."

She gasped; what would Madame say if she were found out? But it would be possible to do it; all the drawers of the bureau were open to her except one, wherein Madame locked secrets of her youth. "Let me read the letter," she told him, and at once he handed her a grubby piece of paper with pencilled writing laboriously achieved round a wood fire. The ashes had streaked the paper.

Dear M. Consett, it read,

I would be more than grateful if you could spare me a few moments of your time to discuss a matter I have very much at heart. I shall be alone on Tuesday, if you were to ride over at any time in the morning. I beg that you keep this secret, and that you will come.

In anticipation,
Emilie Overton.

"And the envelope, too, must be addressed," Dandy Jack assured her. "It is a very little favour, is it not?"

"It might place me in very great danger. It might lose me my place."

"But who is to know that it comes from you? Send it with the ordinary mail, and it will never be seen again by anyone at Withenshaws."

"I do not know—"

"Sidonie, if you will do this thing for me I will give you a guinea for yourself now, and a further guinea after the letter is posted."

"How will you know the letter is posted?" She was beginning to weaken; like most of the French nation, she had a healthy respect for money, and although Madame paid her a fair wage it was not excessive.

"I will know. I know most things. I know, for instance, that you write a very beautiful, neat hand, and do not make blots; and that the letter will look quite different when it is written out again by you on the expensive paper."

"But what will Mr Consett say when he comes to Madame and finds that she did not want to see him at all?"

"They will laugh at it as a little joke. Perhaps it will make them fall in love. Your mistress is dull here, eh?"

Sidonie permitted herself a growing smile which changed to a snort of laughter. "Very well, Dandy Jack, whoever you may be, I'll do it," she said. "But if there's so much as the smell of trouble, I know nothing about it, you understand?"

Nigel laughed also when the letter reached him. He passed it to Sara. "You see, I am at the centre of an intrigue."

Sara frowned. "Do not go, Nigel. Why should she write to you? I have a feeling she did not. Someone else wrote it to get you there."

"But I often ride to Withenshaws."

"Then they do not know when you are coming. Someone wants to get you there at a particular time, and know you will be at a certain place at a certain moment."

"My dear girl, I am not of such importance." He reached out his hand for the letter and stuffed it in his pocket. "You will go, then?" she said.

"I will go, of course. Even if it is a jape she should be told about it, and that someone is using her writing-paper and her name."

She was white with anxiety. "I shall not be at ease till you are home again. Show the letter to Francis and see what he thinks."

"That would be ungallant."

"Oh, you men! You prefer gallantry to common sense any day."

He rose, went to her and kissed her hand with a flourish, as though she had been a French marquise. "That is how I shall treat Mrs Overton," he said. "You are really jealous, you know; that is at the root of all this."

"Oh, Nigel—"

"Well?" He was smiling, the familiar beckoning smile that enabled none to resist him. Perhaps, she thought, the woman really has written. He is enthralling.

"I love you. That is all. Come back safe from Withenshaws."

She knew that she must not become so possessive as to irritate him; that would be the way to lose him. She put on, accordingly, a gay smile, let him kiss her, and all that day went about cheerfully, but it was all pretence. At one point he went with her to the nursery, as he would do daily, to see the children. Sara swooped down and lifted Meri in her arms. The little girl was the plainest of all of them, and must be made a fuss of before she realised it. Nicholas was strutting about beating a toy drum he had had for his birthday. He was strong and sturdy and his hair had stayed curly. Little Dorothy sat now in a chair to which a tray was attached, hemming her in. The doctor had advised that she should not learn to walk too fast, to give her bones time to strengthen. She was docile and good-natured, and sat in the chair without complaining, her curls like those of a cherub. "Francis comes to see her twice and three times a day," Sara said. "He carries her round the room on his shoulder and plays with her as though she were a doll. Is not that so, nurse?" for the starchy-aproned nurse had risen on their entry, and would remain standing until they had gone.

"Oh, yes, madam, he dotes on her. He hardly notices his own son."

But Nicholas, as yet, did not appear to be suffering.

On the Tuesday morning, Nigel rode off on Cloud, making for Withenshaws. Sara had waved him goodbye from the steps, then went up to the window to see him out of sight. At the last corner he turned about in the saddle and waved, knowing she would be there, watching. Her eyes were full of tears and could hardly see him.

And he rade on, and further on,
Wading in red bluid tae the knee.

Where had that come from and why should she think of it now?

They were waiting for him behind the hedges, halfway along the road to Withenshaws; Dandy Jack Runcatch and his brother-in-law Smoker, each carrying a gun. Smoker's was the ordinary kind that any poacher would carry, but Jack had, at the ready, a smooth deadly pistol that had seen service often enough. Hoofbeats sounded along the road. "Be sure it's him and not another," muttered Smoker.

"It's him. What d'ya take me for? Get ready now. If I miss, you shoot. But by God I won't miss."

Nigel came in sight, his dark riding-coat contrasting with the light breeches he wore, his head bare, showing the hair itself lit by the sun. Dandy Jack raised his pistol and fired. Nigel spun about in the saddle, throwing up his hands and at last collapsing forwards. The blood began to spurt out and dye his horse's flank.

"That's a good horse," said Smoker. "We could colour it and sell it up north."

"Don't be a fool. What we do now is get out of here."

But Cloud had in any case turned, and was carrying his dead master back to Ae.

She had shed so many tears she did not think there were more to shed. She had seen them carry Nigel in, lay him on a table and try to find a beat of his heart, his beloved heart that had been shot clean through. She knelt by him, her cheek against his hand, she did not know for how long. "Come away, Sara," said a gentle voice which she did not at first recognise as that of Francis. "You can do nothing for him. None of us can."

So she had gone away, and instead down to the stable, and sobbed against Cloud. "You brought him home," she whispered. "You brought him home." Her tears ran down the animal's sensitive face, channelling at last above his nostrils; once or twice he gave her cheek a little rub, to show he understood. Nigel's blood had seeped beneath the saddle and stained the girths, as well as Cloud's flank. They had already taken off the saddle.

"Come, Sara," said Francis' voice again. "You have his

child to think of." This time he had led her away, and had not left her till she was at the door of her room. Biddy, red-eyed, waited to serve her. "Get your mistress undressed and put her to bed," said Francis curtly. "No, Sara; do as I say."

So she went to bed and lay there, crying always; presently the doctor came up from examining Nigel, and made her drink a draught of laudanum and opium. "That'll get you some sleep, at any rate," he said brusquely. Sara felt the fumes mount to her brain, and struggled out of the rising blankness to ask him a question.

"Yes, we found the bullet. It'll be easy to trace who fired it. Sleep now."

And, obedient at last, she slept; waking many hours later to wonder what heavy weight lay on her heart, and then remembering.

At first the police were suspicious of Francis. What was mere conjecture among the county gossips had filtered down, by way of servants' halls, and one of the maids at Tanbury Hall was walking out with a young constable from Brede. The Force were, therefore, in possession of the facts as they stood; Francis Atherstone had been attached to his cousin's wife, and now the cousin had become attached to *his*; they were like man and wife, the Tanbury Hall maid was understood to have said. Also there had been several tragedies at Withenshaws and Ae, when that family occupied either house. It was true that some were hounded by tragedy; the police knew that as well as anyone. but they came to Ae determined to have it out one way or other with Francis Atherstone.

They were led into his study, with a feeling that they had gone through all this before. "Mr Atherstone?" said the inspector, by way of form. Francis smiled. "Why, yes, inspector; I think we know one another well enough."

"This is a tragic business; tragic, very."

Francis stopped smiling and his face took on the look of a mask made of pale wax. "You have come to ask questions," he said. "I will answer any I may, but I must beg you, if you can, to leave my wife out of this; she is in a delicate condition, and I am keeping her in bed."

"Quite so, sir. We will not disturb Mrs Atherstone unless it becomes urgently necessary; at the present moment there is no need. You were the cousin of the deceased?"

"Our mothers were half-sisters."

"You would know Mr Consett, then, from a boy?"

"From less than that. We were virtually reared together. The only difference between us was that of income. Nigel—Mr Consett—had a substantial fortune of his own, whereas I—" he grimaced—"had to rely on my uncle, who was not fond of parting with his money."

"Yet he left you everything in his will, I believe."

"How do you know that? It is a private matter between myself and the lawyers."

"We have our ways of hearing things, Mr Atherstone; not always when we intend to hear them, but they come in useful."

"Damned useful. You will therefore be acquainted with the conditions of my uncle's will regarding my marriage."

"Something of the sort, sir. In the meantime, your cousin, Mr Consett, the deceased, had been married to the woman you had at one time wished to have as your wife."

"That has nothing to do with his shooting now, I assure you."

"We must explore all avenues, Mr Atherstone. Lady Helena Consett is dead—"

"Damn you, will you stop invoking the past? What has that to do with today's business?"

"It has this, Mr Atherstone; where were you between the hours of ten and half-past eleven on Tuesday, the time when the deceased, as nearly as medical evidence can gather, was shot?"

"I cannot recollect precisely; I do not consult my watch every five minutes. It is possible that I was in the nursery, visiting my grand-niece." He smiled through his anger; the thought of Dorothy was a constant delight.

"Your grand-niece? I was not aware—"

"Or second cousin, or third cousin; I am not certain what she is."

"That is immaterial," said the inspector. "Can you produce evidence that that is where you were during that time?"

"During some of it. I think that for the rest of it I came in here and read. There is, alas, nobody to witness that."

"Then, sir—"

A knock came on the door. It was one of the footmen, who asked if he might have a word with the master. The inspector nodded. "Have your word, and be done. Unless it is of a delicate nature, say it aloud. We shall only have to ask Mr Atherstone concerning it if you do not."

"Sir—Colonel Overton has sent over a message, asking to see you urgently. He says he can clear up this sad business, sir. That was all."

On the carriage-journey, in memory of past days, the inspector asked how Belinda fared.

"She is dead," replied Francis, and vouchsafed no more. He was already irritated with himself for having mentioned Dorothy at all.

The police shook their heads. "Takes 'em in the chest, about that age," said the sergeant, speaking for the first time in history. "Never known one of 'em to see twenty. A mercy, if you look at it that way."

They agreed that it was a mercy, and drove in at the gates of Withenshaws. "Will you allow me, gentlemen," said Francis, "to acquaint my host with the fact that the police are here? If he has solved the mystery of the shooting, he will be glad to see you. But it may be some other matter altogether, in which case I will inform you of it when I come out."

The two officers looked at each other, and agreed. Francis left the carriage and went into the house. Shortly the police were sent for.

They were led to Colonel Overton's study, in which there were three figures; Francis Atherstone, the Colonel himself, and a weeping young woman in lace cap and apron, who kept her chin sunk in her collar.

"Come in, sirs," said the Colonel. "This is a shocking business. Fortunately, I think I can give you a little help—or this young woman can. Dry your eyes, Sidonie; nobody is going to punish you. We were angry, naturally; but you are in no danger."

"They will not send me to prison?" The blubbered face was raised, and the beard revealed itself, to the fascination of the police sergeant.

"I have just made that clear, have I not? Now tell the police exactly what you told me; about your visit to the fair and the man who persuaded you to steal my wife's writing-paper."

Sidonie suddenly launched herself into a volley of rapid French. "That won't do, miss," said the sergeant. "Say what you have to say, but make it in English, even if it's slow. Then I can write it down, see?" They listened while she told her story, slowly; at the end the inspector nodded.

"Dandy Jack Runcatch is an old friend of mine, who's seen the inside of a gaol more than once. Don't you go talking to men like him again, miss, or you might get hurt."

"Runcatch?" said Francis. "Then it was a vendetta. They were out for my cousin's blood in revenge for the earlier Runcatch's hanging."

"Well, now we have this information—we're grateful to you, miss, and to you, Colonel Overton—it'll be only a matter of time before we bring in this other Runcatch, and it won't be healthy for him, I promise you. My apologies, Mr Atherstone, for having detained you so long, but we have to be sure, see?"

In fact, Jack Runcatch was never caught. He had wasted no time in getting himself and Smoker on board ship for Australia; things in this country were getting too hot to hold him, and he could make money wherever he went. For a time, he and Smoker worked on a sheep farm, then tiring of the hard work set up as importers of tea. They did very well, married respectable farmers' daughters, and settled down to continue a line whose origins, however mysterious, went back to the sixteenth century, if not before.

The sad summer passed. In September the news came that Aunt Beatie had died. Sara read the letter absently, with the feeling that it concerned no one she knew. A few days later a letter came from the old lady's lawyers to say that she had left Sara the hundred pounds the latter had repaid her long ago.

"I know what I shall do with it," Sara said to Francis; they were at breakfast. "I shall buy the children a rocking-horse; they have always wanted one, and a life-sized teddy bear."

"If you are going shopping, you had better go soon; and I suppose I should accompany you." She was very heavy with Nigel's child by now; he glanced at her with a kind of sympathy. With Helena gone, there had been room, and time, to grow fond of Sara. He tended to forget the fact that she was his wife. Yes! they would go by easy stages to London, buy the toys, divert Sara, and come home. It came to him, with a kind of amusement at himself, that he wanted to buy a doll for Dorothy; a new-fangled porcelain doll with jointed arms and legs, and eyes that opened and shut, with long lashes.

They found themselves, accordingly, in a famous store which sold nothing but toys. There were bears of all sizes, from the tiny to the huge; Sara selected the biggest one she could see. The rocking-horse was dapple grey, and reminded her of Cloud; she shut her eyes for an instant, and the saleswoman wondered if madam was quite well; her state could be seen even beneath the light cloak she wore. She paid for the two toys, asked for them to be wrapped and taken to the carriage, and looked about to find Francis. He was entranced by a model railway, which ran by itself, with tracks and level crossings. Seeing his absorption in it, she fancied for a moment that she saw Francis the boy; not permitted to have many things of his own, always sharing his richer cousin's. It might well make a child bitter. She went over to him and laid a hand on his arm.

"I have some change, if you would like me to buy it for you," she said. "There would be plenty of room to set it down at Ae."

He smiled, and shook his head. "I have found Dorothy's doll," he told her. "It is being sent up with the other packages."

They travelled home easily, stopping for food at an inn. Sara felt no discomfort from the journey and was touched that Francis so often asked her how she felt. When they had first been married, with Helena constantly near, he would neither have cared to ask nor to think of her.

The children were asleep by the time they reached Ae. Carefully, so that the rustling paper did not wake them, they put the rocking-horse and teddy bear in their places. Francis held on to his wrapped doll. "No," he said to Sara's raised eyebrows. "I want to be with her when she unwraps it, tomorrow."

It struck her, not for the first time, that he doted on Dorothy; in a manner which for so self-contained a man was disquieting.

When Sara's time was drawing near she went to Francis in

his study. Dorothy was there, on the window-seat, her short legs not longer than the width of the cushions, her dimpled hands clutching her doll. Francis would let her sit there by the hour while she nursed it; she never disturbed him. Sara was troubled; it would take Dorothy away from the other children in the nursery, make a stranger of her.

Francis rose when she came in, and drew forward a chair to the fire. While on his feet he swooped Dorothy up in his arms, and the doll too; the child gave a gurgle of pleasure. She had just begun to say her first words. She nestled against Francis' waistcoat, her long lashes drooping on her cheeks.

"I have been wondering," Sara said, "whether we are accursed because we are flying in the face of truth."

"My dear girl, what an extraordinary statement! Explain it to me."

"Do you deny that we are accursed, after all that has been?"

He frowned, picked up Dorothy's doll by the jointed wrist and played with it. "Perhaps the others were," he admitted, "Nigel, Helena, Belinda, poor Mary Bartlett."

"And we are left with the curse on our heads. Francis, I have been thinking this over very carefully, and I do not want you to be angry with me or think me a light-headed woman when I tell you of it. You received all the money from your uncle's will, did you not?"

He flushed. "Yes, but—"

"Including the second instalment which was to be yours when I bore you a living son?"

"Sara, that is begging the question. I *have* a son, and—"

"And a daughter, whom I bore you. Your son Mary Bartlett bore you. I do not doubt that Nicholas is your son; he is very like you in features if not in nature. Meri we can set aside. The child I lost that day on the ice would have fulfilled the agreement, but did not."

"All this is useless talk." He frowned, and went to the sideboard where there stood a bottle of madeira. He poured her a glass, but she shook her head.

"I am not taking wine till this child is born. I want him to be alive and healthy more than I have ever wanted anything, Nigel's son. After that—Francis, I will bear you a living son if I can, and if you will."

He had turned to stare at her. "Sara—I think—" He set the glass down without drinking from it, came back to his place, and stood kicking the fender. "I—I have not been good to you," he said.

"You are better now. We know each other better. And we have both loved others, and know it. Children have been conceived under less happy circumstances. Think what it would be like to have your own legitimate son, to take your name. It need not make you love the rest—" her glance dwelt on Dorothy, set aside in the chair—"any less. But . . . this is difficult for me . . . it would mean that you are entitled to the money, which if I know you you have half spent."

He laughed. "Yes, I did spend it; most of it on wine and women."

"I was certain of that, but it does not concern me. It is only that—that we are living a lie, I as well as you, and I cannot have a quiet conscience until the matter is righted."

He spread out his hands, staring at his signet ring. Suddenly he smiled. "Wait, at least," he told her, "till this one is born. I am as anxious to see him as you are. Afterwards . . . we can discuss it again."

By that she knew that he had agreed to it. If only she might live through this birth!

She lived, though it was a difficult labour and the doctor

advised no more children for at least a year. The child was a boy. He did not look like Nigel; he had a huge intelligent head, great square fists which he clenched like a pugilist, and an adult leer which was perceptible as soon as his eyes were open. "I know who he is like!" cried Sara when she was able. "He is like Dad! He will grow up into a potter or sculptor; that is a potter's thumb. I never thought that I should feel happy again; I almost dreaded that he would look like Nigel and remind me always of grief; but now—"

"What will you call him?" enquired Francis, who privately considered the latest arrival to be the ugliest infant he had ever seen.

"Alexander. Oh, it is nobody's name. But he will be like nobody . . . except himself."

"Some talk of Alexander, and some of Hercules," prophesied Francis solemnly.

As Alexander grew it became evident that he did not want to take away Nicholas' drum, or everybody's teddy bear, or stay on the rocking horse all day. Sara gave him lumps of soft putty to play with, and at an early age he would make them into little animals, cows or dogs or sheep. "Make a person," cried Meri, who often watched him and had he been older would have been his devoted servitor. "I can't yet," replied Alexander. "People fall down."

Dorothy was seldom in the nursery. They had grown accustomed to her coming back at bedtime, having spent all day downstairs. It did not occur to them to resent this; they had always been used to it. Dorothy was in some way different from all of them, never lost her temper, never screamed or cried or called anyone names. It was like sharing the night-nursery with a very good wax doll who would go to sleep at once.

Sara became pregnant by Francis three years after Alexander's birth. Waiting had been bitter; the conception itself had not been easy, lacking love on either side; they had both been embarrassed, and several attempts had come to nothing, and she had had to persuade him more than once to try again, like a child; but at last the good news came, and after that she, who had seldom prayed, never missed a single night of prayer that it should be a boy. She went out seldom, working in her garden, or playing quietly with the children; if visitors came she would entertain them courteously, but refused invitations. Even a carriage-ride was a risk; she would not take it. Francis chided her and told her to enjoy herself more. "You can't spend nine months cooped up at Ae," he said. "*I* should go mad."

"Perhaps I always was mad. You go off to London for a week or two. And it isn't nine months now, it's six."

Sometimes, when it was not too cold, she would go down to the pottery and take Alexander with her. He attacked the clay almost before she showed him how to treat it, the magical ox-head and wringing and wedging. She let him see the wheel at work and he watched, fascinated, while the cylinder rose and fell and rose again. "Now," said his mother, "do you want a flower pot or a bowl?"

"Flower pot. Then I can grow a tomato in it. Nurse is always growing tomatoes. And geraniums, but I don't like those, they're silly."

"You talk too much," she told him. "Potters never talk

while they work, otherwise it doesn't come out properly. Look what you've made me do to this one; the clay's spoiled. Now, just for that, you wedge the new clay next and then you can throw it on the wheel."

He was far too short, of course, to kick the lower wheel while the upper rotated, and she set him on a stool and kicked for him, while his hands, uncertain at first, got the clay under control. "No, get the potter's grip—inside with your left hand, outside with your right. The right shapes the rim and later we tidy it. No, don't squash down, lift up, up, up." Finally she taught him; and taught him also the feeling of tired clay, so that although all he had made that day was a tiny little pot, he would improve, then nobody would stop him.

Meribah felt left out of things. She was not interested in clay or drums, although when she was smaller she had used to talk to the teddy bear. He was well worn now and had lost an eye. Mama would come and talk to her sometimes and tell her she was going to be pretty, and so would have to have good manners as well. "Everybody notices a pretty face, but if the person behind it is unpleasant they don't take any more notice," Meribah was told, and Nurse endorsed these statements. So Meri tried to be well-mannered as well as pretty, although she did not see how she could be the latter, with her straight black hair. The princesses in fairy tales always had golden curls, like Dorothy. Having had this confided to her one day, Sara unearthed a set of ribbons.

"We will do your hair the French way, and then you will see how interesting it can be," the child was told. "First of all we take a comb—there—and divide everything into four. Then we make two plaits at the front, which you must hold, while I make two more at the back. Then we loop them over the side of your head, and tie them tight with the ribbons. Now you are a little French girl, very *chic*."

"What's *chic*?" Meribah gazed at herself in the mirror and saw a transformed stranger, almost as, she told herself, she would look when she was grown up.

"*Chic* is always wearing the right clothes, and being in the right place, and saying the right things, and being witty to make people laugh, but never, *never* to hurt anybody." Sara was unsure whether or not a French dictionary would have agreed with her, but it would do to go on with. Meribah laughed; she had pretty white teeth and seldom showed them. Care must be taken, her mother thought, that she did not grow up sullen, like Francis.

Suddenly she herself sat back and laughed. Long ago she had been ejected from a dame school because she had no way with children, and had smitten Willie Something-or-other on the bottom. It was different now. How she wished the next child were born!

He was a boy. He weighed nine pounds, was healthy, vociferous, and had curly hair like Nicholas. In fact he resembled Nicholas in many ways. She lay in bed happier than she had been since Nigel died, and heard Francis come into the room to see his son. He bent over her, kissed her, and asked how she was.

"Never mind me. Look at *him*. You shall choose the name this time."

"Wasn't there something about Saul having slain his thousands, but David his ten thousands? Let's call him David."

David slept.

Sara had become something of a recluse of late years; the children and her pottery took up most of her time, and when Francis was away she did not accompany him. Yet even he left Ae less and less; he seemed entirely contented with his books and Dorothy.

The children had a dancing-master from the time they were six years old. When it came to Dorothy's turn to join the class she took to it naturally; Mr Powell said afterwards to Sara that he hardly needed to teach her. She was like a fairy, drifting above the floor, her golden curls flying; they were long enough now to reach her waist. The resemblance to Helena had become more and more obvious, but Dorothy was warmer in nature than her grandmother; almost, she seemed to echo poor Belinda's delighted smiles and laughter at any small thing. Francis was enchanted with her. To please him, Sara sent for pattern books from the fashion-houses and had the local dressmaker run up pretty clothes for Meribah and Dorothy; she herself was not interested and usually appeared in the rusty old black dress in which she did her gardening.

As for the boys, they loathed the dancing-class, especially Alexander, who seemed to have been born with two left feet. Nicholas, on the other hand, pirouetted gracefully. "I think he sees himself already at the regimental ball," said Sara to Francis, after one of their rare views of the class taking place; generally they left it to the master and his fiddler, an old man whom he took about with him because every house did not have a pianoforte. The old man played quadrilles and reels well, and could also launch forth into a waltz; Sara would feel proud of her fashionable young ladies when at last she took them to the Assembly at Brede. As for Nicholas, he had wanted to be a soldier ever since he understood what the word meant; so there would be no difficulty in choosing a career for him. Sara knew what Alexander would be, but had said little of it yet in case Francis was displeased. One day he called her into his study.

"Sit down, my dear. I wanted to tell you what I have put in my will regarding you and the children. Some of it may surprise you, but I hope on the whole it will please you."

"It is your affair, Francis." She fingered the leather arms of the chair. "I came to you with nothing, to paraphrase the saying, and I expect to take nothing out."

"It is not quite so bad as that. I would have left you the house if I could, but as you know, it is entailed. I have, however, left you the liferent of it, and enough to live on and buy yourself some new clothes, now and again, although I know you will spend the money on clay."

"A kiln, I think," she said. "It is kind of you, Francis."

"The house itself, and the farms, will be David's. I have written a covering letter to the lawyer explaining our various family complexities. I should like to see his face when he spells them out, but I won't. The remainder of the money, apart from what I have left to yourself, I have divided amongst all the children except Dorothy."

"Except Dorothy? I thought she was your favourite."

"She is."

"Then—"

"Do not ask me now," he said. "Later I will tell you more certainly what I plan. Do the other arrangements please you?"

"More than I can say. It is good of you to include Alexander."

"I like the little ruffian. Besides, if he is going to be a sculptor he will have no money from the fruits of his toil. Sculptors and painters are never recognised until they are dead. I have left him enough to buy himself a long loaf of French bread and a glass of absinthe on the South Bank."

"And David?"

"David will be the squire. I must begin to take him with me when I go round the estate. As for you, you must bring Meribah out and get her married. In due course we must have a ball."

"It is a little early. She is only a child."

"I want her to get to know other children. She is kept too closely here."

Sara gave a children's party, and then another; and found herself deluged with return invitations, all of which she must accept or else the children would be broken-hearted, and each one of which she must attend to chaperone her brood. She grew weary of it, and of the inane talk of the other mothers; but she held her own, and the legend that Mrs Atherstone was uncouth again gradually died its death. How long ago it seemed that she had driven out wilfully to the *fête champêtre*! And how Francis had changed!

They had not continued as lovers after David's birth; each of them recognised that it had been only for that necessity and that their hearts were elsewhere. One day Nurse came to Sara in a state of perturbation.

"Madam, may I have a word with you in private?" She was always correct, starchy, reliable, and with a good knowledge of childish illness. Sara went with her to where they could talk alone.

"Madam, it's Miss Dorothy. She's not so old yet, but I think, if I may say so, that for her to sleep in Mr Atherstone's dressing-room is not proper."

"Sleep in his dressing-room?" said Sara, amazed. "How long has this been happening?"

"It has not happened yet, madam, but the order came today. Her clothes and toys are to be moved down there and it is to be made into a room of her own."

"You were right to tell me," said Sara. Later she confronted Francis. "What does it mean?" she said, more sharply than usual. "Nurse is upset, and with reason."

"It means that I give orders in my own house, and if Nurse dislikes them she can go elsewhere."

"Francis, you know very well that she is a treasure and we are fortunate to have her."

"Then she can do as she is told."

The things were moved down, even Dorothy's little white-painted bed. Sara changed the curtains to gingham and gave out the discreet story that Dorothy was kept awake in the nursery with the other children. No one believed it; and the state of affairs worried Sara. It was not so very long now until Dorothy would reach puberty. She prayed that something would happen to alter the arrangement by then. As for Nurse, it was in any case time to change to a tutor: this was accomplished without calamity.

Time passed, and the years. One day Colonel Overton came to Ae.

He seemed embarrassed, and Sara chaffed hin; they were old enough friends now for her to do this. Francis was at home, and the three of them sat in his study drinking madeira.

"Truth to tell," the Colonel said, "it's my wife who made me come. 'Come with me,' I said, but she told me to my face it's a man's business to deal with men—no offence to you, ma'am," he said hastily. "It's my son," he said. "He was mightily taken with Miss Meribah at the Hunt Ball. He had no eyes for anyone else all night."

Sara looked pleased. She was remembering Meri in her pretty white gown, trimmed with old French lace that had belonged to some ancestress at Ae. Long ago Meri had wanted to be *chic*, and *chic* she was, if not pretty. She never lacked for partners at any mixed assembly. She was a quiet girl, but whatever she said was correct. She will, thought Sara who knew very well what was coming, make a good army wife. Young Overton was a cadet at Woolwich, in his final year.

"—and so, I promised that I would ride over and sound you both. There is one thing—" He flushed a beetroot colour, and wiped his brow with a spotless handkerchief. "I do not know how I *can* ask you this without offence, but there's been talk, and although one doesn't heed it, there it is, and—"

"I know what you want to know," said Sara steadily. "I can give you my word of honour, and Francis' also, that Meribah is his daughter and mine. Do you remember, Francis? You called her Waters of Bitterness because you so wanted a son."

"Which I have since got," said Francis smoothly. "No need to worry, Colonel Overton; if anyone else has a query, send 'em to me."

"Feel a fool to have mentioned it," said the Colonel. "This is very excellent madeira. At first, of course, they wouldn't have much to live on, none of the young officers have, but later—"

"Meribah will have a little money of her own later also," Francis said.

"Do not you think," Sara interposed, "that before we settle it we should give him a chance to *ask* her?"

Meribah and young Lieutenant Overton were married in the parish church a year later, when the bridegroom had completed his passing-out with distinction. He was a handsome boy, with a broad suntanned brow beneath the magnificent dress uniform cap; one could see him in later years as a brigadier. The couple were to live in army quarters at first, and soon expected to be posted abroad. "Though with all this rumbling over South Africa, it may be nearer than we expect—or want," said Mrs Overton, magnificent in a hat with a sweeping brim embellished with ospreys, and a dove-coloured gown a trifle too young for her figure. Sara wore green.

Everybody was talking about South Africa, just as, a short while ago as it seemed, they had talked about Sebastopol. It had not seemed then that that could in any way affect life here, with the glorious summer they were having.

Dorothy had been the bridesmaid, and afterwards, at the reception, swung round the floor partnered by Francis; they danced as one. Her hair had been put up for the occasion and she was uncannily like Helena. The older men and women present murmured about it, but none asked a direct question; it would have been difficult to frame. Sara would always remember Dorothy's swinging blue skirts and massed golden hair, and Francis's tall figure with the dark hair just turning, at the temples, to grey. Had Helena ever danced with him so, when they were young?

London, 4th August

My dear Sara,

By the time that you receive this, it will be too late to stop the course of events. I do not mean the war, about which everyone is unreasonably jubilant here; war is an ugly fact, not an occasion for rejoicing.

I am writing to tell you certain things that may shock and grieve you, but they must be told; as you yourself once said, we must not fly in the face of truth. The truth is that Dorothy has been my mistress since she was fourteen years old. She has more than replaced Helena for me, and I thought that I could never love anyone more than Helena; but we never loved in the flesh. Dorothy and I love one another so deeply, and always have, that the words 'one flesh' are for me taken out of the marriage service and placed here, in my hand, and in hers holding it. No one has ever known her very well except myself.

You may ask, why go away? Why take the step we are now taking? It is not only that I, as a man over age, would be useless in the war; I suppose I could lie about my age; others have. The fact is that Dorothy is pregnant. I tried not to let this happen during all the times we have been together; but it has happened, and now we must ask ourselves what kind of child she might bear? Her mother was a mongol and her father a sadistic gipsy. I would dread the future for her if I thought that she would live.

As it is—you have already guessed it—we are taking the way we both think is best, for I have told her the truth also. You will do without me at Ae very well.

Farewell, my dear. Forgive me, if you can, all the unhappiness I caused you at the beginning and the final grief—for it will be so—I am causing you now. In the holocaust that is coming our deaths will hardly be remembered, although for a little while there may be headlines in the newspapers.

The will is in order, as I outlined it to you; and you are free.

Ever your devoted
Francis.

The man and girl were found dead in bed in a London hotel, in the attitude of love. Beside them was an empty bottle of laudanum and two glasses. Everyone but Sara blamed the coming of war.

There was surprisingly little difference at Ae. Nicholas joined up at once; Meri, whose husband had been sent abroad with the first consignment, came back to live with her mother; Alexander spent his time in the pottery and ate snatched meals. David, the squire now, rode about the estate as Francis had done. Sara began to think of turning Ae into a hospital; it was not large enough to take wounded, but it might suit convalescents very well. She began to attend Red Cross classes at Brede, taking Meri with her. There was plenty of help; by the end of the year Ae was a convalescent hospital, efficiently run.

The time went by. Alexander was old enough to join up, but would not go; he said he was a conscientious objector. To see the strong, unhurt young man beside the maimed thin souls who came in caused a kind of revulsion in Sara; but in her heart she agreed with her son; war was evil. Later, Alexander had to appear before a tribunal; white feathers were handed to him in the streets.

Worse was to come. Nicholas was killed at Spion Kop, Meri's husband at Ladysmith. One day Sara came down to find Meri and Alexander having bitter words. "He is killed—all those fine men are killed—and you stay here playing with clay. I do not think that I can stay under the same roof with you any longer; I will tell Mama."

"I am here," said Sara, "and you will do as you must."

Meri suddenly broke down and began to weep. "If Brian and I had had a child it would not be so bad—but I have no one. And so many women are like me."

She found a vacant place in one of the V.A.D. detachments at St. Albans and stayed there for the rest of the war

After she had gone Alexander grew restless. He no longer troubled to make pots; he would sit for hours, silent and brooding, in front of the wood fire in the part of the house they had kept as their private quarters. "I know what is troubling you," Sara said. "It is something you must decide for yourself; but why not go out with a Red Cross detachment? That way you would not have to fight."

He went, and had his right arm blown off by an unexploded mine while carrying in stretchers from the battlefield.

Alexander came home three weeks after the war ended. She had been prepared for almost any change in him, despair, the sullens, anything; but that he should be exactly the same was almost shocking.

He sat by the fire and they drank tea, while he talked all the time. He said they were going to fit him with an artificial arm "and, don't you see, if one had to go, it was much better to be the right? I can still use the wheel and shape the rim with whatever hook they give me—in fact it'll be like a tool—and my left hand is as good as it ever was, to shape up with. They say the blind grow an extra sense of feel and touch in an amazingly short time, and that's how I feel. First of all I'm going to build you the best kiln that's ever been built, and then, Mama, you and I are going to have an exhibition. These poor fellows still upstairs won't stop me getting started; in fact there's one who's offered to help with the kiln. He's lost a leg, but he can handle bricks."

She listened to him talk with amazement, aware of his

dynamism; it had come, she knew, from herself. When she was his age she had been chafing against the restrictions of Aunt Beatie's dame-school and Miss Edgeworth's shop—and contracted a mad marriage that wouldn't happen today; that will would have been contested, she thought. But did she regret it, and Nigel's love? Never. Nor did she regret the kind of courage Alexander was showing, not because he wanted to make an impression but because he was being himself. Courage wore two faces, of war and peace.

The kiln was finished in a fortnight and those convalescents who were still on the premises and were not too badly wounded to offer, said they would take watches to fire the wood overnight. Sara had a good deal of greenware pottery on hand, and explained its brittleness to the men as it was packed carefully by herself into the shelved kiln; afterwards, she said, it would be hard but porous, not holding water. They listened politely and when, two days later, the fired and cooled kiln was carefully opened, appeared uninterested in the pinkish biscuit forms. But Sara took them in and glazed them, and filled the kiln again, explaining that this time it must hold much less; not one piece must touch another or both would be ruined. "And the colours that come out are different from those that went in," she said. "Sometimes we get surprises . . . and sometimes almost a miracle, and can't remember how we mixed it."

She let them lift a turf when the kiln was at full heat, to see the shining of the melting glaze. When it had been through full firing and had cooled she opened the turves with a sense of excitement that was never absent from a glost firing; what would one find? There were copper greens and dulled blues, the latter having come with mixing manganese with cobalt, and an elusive yellow from a recipe of Sara's own. "When you goin' to write a book, nurse?" they asked her; she was always nurse to them. "Never," she said. "Until I die I hope I can stay on here, doing just this; it's what I've wanted to do all my life, and though other things got in the way I always kept on with it, sometimes a little, sometimes a lot. It means making something out of nothing; taking the clay that's fined down from old, old rock and pushing it together again to make what it came from. To me, that's a way of living; but not for everyone."

"It's interestin', but give me a night at the Palladium," said the man who had helped to fire the wood. Alexander laughed. He had grown a short beard, which made him look more than ever eccentric and like a potter. He was impatient for the arrival of his metal arm, then he would start also to make wheel pottery; just now, all he could do, besides the rough work of the kiln, was to carve blocks of clay with his left hand. He had already made interesting abstract shapes with these; they were not yet dry enough to fire. "What you need's patience," he had said to a boy who had lost half his face, and wanted to learn. He sounded callous, but was not. He taught the boy, shouted at him, cursed him, then after many failures saw him at last turn out a perfect pot. Then he hugged him with his single arm. "I knew you were a potter," he said. "You'll never give up now."

Sara went upstairs after placing the newly glazed ware on its shelf and looked at herself in the mirror. She saw a stoutish woman with grey hair, face streaked with whiting from the glazes, and happy green eyes. A voice from the far past said *It's so unladylike, and the aprons are never the same again.*

It didn't matter.